OLD

JEWELS

This is a work of fiction. Names, characters, places, and incidents either are the product of the author's imagination or are used fictitiously, and any resemblance to actual persons living or dead, events, or locales is entirely coincidental.

Copyright © 2016 Pat Pratt

Publisher: Pat Pratt Publishing

ISBN: 978-0-9980790-0-4 (Paperback)
ISBN: 978-0-9980790-1-1 (EBook)

A big *Thank You* goes out to all who stuck with me through all the starts and stops of this book.

To my friends and family, who kept asking, here it is. You are too many to name individually, but you know who you are.

To my critiquing group, *Write On*, your encouragement and suggestions helped make this work far better than it ever could have been without you.

Special thanks to my granddaughter, *Jennifer Gann*, who can, with the click of a button, whip my computer into submission when it stands up and defies me.

And finally, from this computer-challenged senior citizen, a great big thank you to *Anita Dickason*, who managed to get this manuscript from my flash drive to the finished product.

I hope you all enjoy reading as much as I did the writing.

God Bless
Pat Pratt

Chapter 1

Let Me Introduce Myself

I don't know quite where to begin with an introduction, I've never written a book before. The whole book idea started as a little newsletter highlighting residents at Golden Harvest, the retirement village where I reside. Writing a book was the last thing on my mind; but my friends told me I should compile an account of how we helped catch the thieves who were preying upon the residents of the establishment. I wrote it all down, but was convinced none of it would ever see the light of day. If it hadn't been for—but I'm getting ahead of myself. I need to start at the beginning, which, I guess, would be to explain how I ended up at Golden Harvest in the first place.

My name is Helen Boyer-Patterson, and I am a relatively healthy, relatively happy septuagenarian. Being seventy-plus years old allows a person a bit of independence and eccentricity. I enjoyed that independence and lived, perfectly content, in my home, a two-story semi run-down old mausoleum in my childhood hometown of Loblolly, Georgia. The house was paid for, a legacy from my parents; but, I must admit, it was getting more and more difficult to keep the drafty old place going. Even with a once-a-

1

week cleaning lady, the day-to-day upkeep was a chore. One day as I descended the old staircase, I tripped on the frayed stair runner and rolled my five-foot-ten, 245-plus bulk, not too gracefully, to the floor below and broke my left hip.

After the surgery I was removed to a rehabilitation prison where I had to work myself toward parole. I was poked and prodded and probed by physical therapists, mental therapists, social conscience therapists, and every other manner of 'ists', during the course of my incarceration. It was in no way, shape or form, an enjoyable experience for a seventy-year-old confirmed loner used to making the rules, not abiding by them.

I was forced to withstand the tortures of the sadistic physical therapist. He told me to call him Russell, but I think he received his credentials at the Gestapo School of Therapy. His torturous methods were more in line with someone named Wolfgang Zybo. I have always abhorred exercise in all forms, except swimming, which I indulge in as often as possible. The buoyancy I attain in the water lifts my spirits—not to mention my considerable bulk. No matter that I may resemble a beached whale; in the water I can float aimlessly and, for a short time at least, experience the freedom of near-weightlessness. Unfortunately, there were no pool privileges in store for me under Dr. Zybo's care. Every day I rowed, walked, pedaled and stretched on torturous machines, and at the end of each session had made no forward progress.

"What's the point?" I asked him. "We're doing all this moving and going absolutely nowhere!"

He replied, "Is for to make you strong."

Those may not have been his exact words, but that's what I heard! Still, I continued my rowing, peddling and treading, in hopes I'd find my way upstream soon.

Some of the people who were there, as I was, for rehabilitation, if not completely ambulatory, were somewhat articulate. Such was not the case with others with whom I came in contact. Sharing a room with some poor soul with unknown maladies and a TV that droned day and night was bad enough, but sitting across the dinner table from imperfect strangers raised my gastric juices to explosive acidic levels.

I requested that my meals be served to me in my room, but evidently there is a rule at the establishment that, unless an inmate is bed-ridden, meals must be taken in the general dining area.

I spoke to my daughter, Emily, about the problem on one of her infrequent visits. She talked to the head nurse and reported back to me, "Mother, social interaction is recommended for the healing process. Don't be obstinate! It won't hurt you to sit and chit chat with other people." She patted my hand, "Be a good girl and go eat your lunch."

"Just who is the mother around here?" I certainly was not ready to relinquish that role to her yet. "Besides," I reminded her, "I don't like to chit chat. And," I added, rubbing my stomach for effect, "I think the ordeal is giving me ulcers. You are not the one in danger of receiving a milk bath when some shaky old person miscalculates her reach and knocks over her drink into your lap."

"Oh, Mother," she huffed, "quit being so dramatic."

Against my wishes, and my better judgment, I returned to the dining room for my meals. But I put in a request for a table alone, on the pretext that I was a writer contemplating a novel and didn't want to be disturbed.

I never managed to row or pedal out of the place, but I was

finally paroled from The Bighouse for good behavior. I breathed a sigh of relief that my troubles were finally over.

Unfortunately, I soon found out they had only just begun.

Chapter 2

The Old Woman Didn't Know What to Do-
Her Children Were Driving Her Cuckoo

My well-meaning children coerced my doctor to tell me I was not to return to my aforementioned lifestyle, bless their little hearts. I love my four children, and some of them actually admit to the family ties, too.

My youngest, Aaron, is, for all intents and purposes, homeless. He hauls a thirty-six-foot travel trailer around behind his one-ton pickup, and anywhere he parks it is home. He works as a fabricator/welder on water towers and high-rises—the higher the better. It's difficult to carry on a conversation with him, he's always so upbeat and happy-go-lucky. It must be due to the extended periods of lack of oxygen to his brain from being so high in the air. I called him about my pending eviction from my home. "Aaron, you aren't talking to me from the top of some half-finished building, are you?"

"No, Mom. I told you, I don't use my cell phone when I'm in the air—usually. But I get a really good signal up here—uh, there. I mean, I would if I actually made calls from up that high. You worry too much, Mom. I've never broken my neck. The view is awesome

5

from the air. I feel close to my Creator up here."

"Yeah, that's what all those people said about the Tower of Babel, and look where it got them!" I argued. "Besides, technically, I created you, and I don't even like heights. Never mind, that's not why I called. I just wanted to ask you a simple question. Did you agree with Emily that I should be forced out of my home?"

"Yeah, well, it's a good idea. Hope you like living in the new place, Mom. Sorry I won't be there to help you pack, but could you put my rock star figures in a safe place, please? Gotta go, I'm losing your signal. Love you."

He has always marched to the beat of a different drummer. So far he's kept ahead of his creditors and his maker, for which I'm grateful. But I wish he would light someplace long enough to have a return address.

My middle son, Michael, is a workaholic. He owns a cabinet-making business, works for another guy, and spends his spare time landscaping his yard. His work ethic is amazing - and exhausting. He didn't get that gene from his father—or me either, for that matter. I like to stay busy, but I'm not as driven as he is.

Since he's into carpentry, I asked if he could fix up my place so it would be safe for me to stay there.

"The place is a money pit, Mom. The cost would eat up every cent you have. But I'll give you an estimate if you insist. Let's see, I have some free time in July—of next year."

He wouldn't loan me his truck, but did offer to help haul what little I could take with me to my new place—if he could work it into his schedule. I guess that's something.

My oldest son, Steve, the computer programmer, began to

speak another language at age twelve. He got a paper route and invested his earnings in his first computer, paying it out over a period of time at the local Radio Shack. When he was young I tried to pick up computer-speak to let him know I took an interest in what he considered important.

"What do you mean, your mother's bored?" I asked. "I'm not bored; I do lots of things to keep busy. You should speak to that Ike. Who is he and why is he on top of the desk?"

"No, Mom," Steve corrected, shaking his head, "it's Mother board—B-O-A-R-D. It's like memory for the computer. And Ike is not a name. It's an icon—I-C-O-N—on the desk top." He pointed to what looked like a portable TV screen. "This is a monitor—we call that a desk top."

"What does it monitor?" I checked my watch. "It's almost time for the news. Can you turn the monitor to channel 5?"

"No, Mom. It's not a TV."

"No soap operas, either, I suppose."

He squeezed his eyes shut, rubbed his temples and sighed, "No, Mom."

I have learned a lot since then, but to this day, I still hardly understand a word he says. Even answers to simple, everyday questions are filled with computer-speak. To my query about being railroaded into a retirement home he mumbled things like, "You'll 'escape' the worry of house upkeep, 'delete' the necessity of bill paying, and your 'mouse' problem will be eliminated." I'm surprised he didn't find a way to use 'caps lock' or 'system requirements' in his recitation.

Which brings me to Emily—The Enforcer. I'm sure she instigated the idea that I wasn't capable of living in my own home any longer. She has the misguided notion that I need to be looked after like an errant child, and plays her 'martyred for mom' role to the hilt with her brothers. She also has the obnoxious traits of always needing to have the last word, and always having to be right about everything. I have no idea where she got those genes—probably from her father.

She convinced the doctor and her brothers that, since my home was old, cold and drafty and had that treacherous, hip-breaking staircase, another fall might do me in. Of course, she left it to the doctor to lower the boom on my living arrangements. She inherited that gene from her father, too—avoid confrontation with Mom at all costs; let someone else do the dirty work. And then she could come in and do damage control.

"Mother," she said as she hugged me, "I know how you love the old homestead. But I've talked to the boys and we all agree Doctor Hanson is right."

Ever cautious when my daughter offers hugs, I pushed her away and braced myself for her argument. "I'll be fine at home."

"I'm sure you would be, but the doctor says that's not an option."

I crossed my arms defiantly across my chest. "I suppose *you* are going to tell me what my options are, then?"

"Well," she smiled, "we thought Golden Harvest Retirement Village would be a perfect solution. Aunt Maggie lives there, and you two would be able to visit every day."

My offspring had always addressed my oldest and dearest friend, Maggie Taylor, as Aunt Maggie. Emily continued, undaunted by my stare. "I made an appointment for us to go check it out today. Aunt Maggie said she'd show us around."

My darling daughter figured I'd accept the move without giving the family too much grief since Maggie had already settled in there. I grudgingly allowed her to escort me to the place; I was convinced nothing would come of it.

Maggie showed us around and introduced me to people whose names I had no intention of remembering since I wasn't staying. My daughter had covered all her bases. She had made an appointment for us to discuss finances with George Hardestee, another old friend, who happened to be the administrator at Golden Harvest. Emily, being in real estate, knew the value of my house and informed us at the interview that she already had someone lined up to buy it out from under me. I found myself, like my youngest son, homeless, so I opted to make the move.

The transition went as smoothly as can be expected for one forced to consolidate seventy years of living into an apartment-sized life. On the upside, I have only one bill to pay, and Maggie is here. I must admit, I'm glad to have her around, but even best friends get on your nerves sometimes.

Chapter 3

All The World's a Headline

I am, as I said, a loner; I am also a people watcher. I began writing little sketches about the characters here in Golden Harvest Retirement Village as an excuse to not get involved with Maggie and her incessant activities. The only other time I attempted writing was a column for my college newspaper, The Observer. You know the sort, columns like it appear in every high school and college rag. Not as outlandish as the newsstand rubbish, but close. Things like: "Guess what short dark-haired cutie was seen in the arms of someone whose initials are G.W." I considered myself the Hedda Hopper of the sorority crowd.

So it seems I've come full-circle back to my youth—to close-quarters, lack of privacy, living in the midst of people who can't think further than what's for lunch—people who fight for the largest piece of pie or the best Bingo card. From the state college to the State of Perpetual Confusion called Golden Harvest.

The name suggests a place Jason and the Argonauts should be exploring, or shearing the golden sheep for its golden fleece. No such luck. Golden Harvest is for people in various stages of aging that range from the mildly decrepit to full-blown senility.

Very little exploring gets done here, except for an occasional pair of misplaced eyeglasses—or in Gladys Butler's case, her dentures. The missing teeth were later discovered in Charlie Arbuckle's medicine chest. How? Some questions a lady does not ask. "Whose pearly whites were found between the aspirins and corn pads in C.A.'s room?" would not be an appropriate lead-in to my next news story.

But I digress. Golden Harvest Retirement Village is not really a village; we don't have a mayor or our own post office. Around here it is sometimes referred to as the Over-the-Hilton—an upscale hotel atmosphere of apartments for seniors. The ratio of women to men is similar to most geographical areas, which means there are a lot more old women than old men. For my purposes that's great; women, of any age, are much more talkative than men. These folks are real characters, more interesting to write about than flighty college girls—if you can keep them from discussing their bodily functions. And it beats Bingo. So I began writing stories on my computer about the residents here, printed them out and sent them to my family in place of newsy letters about my general complaints and ailments.

Marvelous invention, the computer. I can finally see what so fascinates my son about it. My granddaughter brought me the machine, and even took me to computer classes at the community college. Ellyn, Steve's daughter, naturally, is a sweet girl, but is always trying to push me into enjoying some fool thing or another, under the pretense of, "Granny, it's good to stimulate your mind. It will help keep you young." What young people don't understand is that old people have already been young; maybe now we want to sit back and be old.

I took to the computer, though. I can be a curmudgeon and still like the computer. It's a powerful tool. Cut. Paste. And especially DELETE.

The exercise ballooned into the newsletter, which I dubbed 'The Harvester'. At times, some of the residents might take offense, but the truth must be told; we commentators owe it to our reading public. And it doesn't cost them a cent. If there's anything these old folks like better than Bingo, it's something free!

The newsletter became the springboard for my friends and me to solve the crime at Golden Harvest. I'm not saying the Feds wouldn't have figured it out eventually, but they couldn't deny our help was invaluable in catching the criminals.

Chapter 4

Settling In or Settling For

I'm not really too discontented here at Golden Harvest. It's not all that bad. It's actually a nice little retirement home—Retirement *Village*, the brochure says. The apartments are cozy, with little kitchenettes sporting microwaves and mini appliance. Tiny refrigerators hold a quart of milk or a six-pack of drinks, but not at the same time. Playhouse-sized ice cube trays rest in shoebox freezers. All we lack are the oversized hats, high heels and mud pies to remind us we have come full circle back to the playhouses of our childhood.

The apartments have similar floor plans, although Maggie's is a mirror image of mine. To the right inside my front door is an alcove that my granddaughter, Ellyn, keeps trying to decorate for me. Last Christmas she set up an artificial Christmas tree there, but most of the time the corner's only decoration is a floor lamp and a small table where I drop my keys when I come inside. To the left is a walk-in closet/storage area where the residents can store all the excesses of their scaled-down lives. I keep my off-season clothes and that infernal artificial tree in there.

Past the overflow closet on the left is the small el that serves as the kitchen. I have an apartment size table and four chairs there, although I have no intention of serving meals to anyone.

Behind that, part of the same room, is my computer desk that sits against the side wall by the door to the patio; from there I can work and watch people coming and going. The remainder of my living area consists of a couple of overstuffed chairs, a small couch, all cozily situated around the window and patio door.

On the right side is the bathroom with access from the main living area or from my bedroom that is tucked in the back corner. The place is not exactly the Taj Mahal, but is serviceable. The whole apartment is not much larger than my master bedroom at home, and I had to do some serious downsizing when I moved here. I sometimes miss the space, but I can't say I miss that staircase or the drafts from the old homestead.

Dining facilities are available for real meals, and lawns are attended by grounds-keepers. Most of us aren't decrepit or senile—at least not entirely. A few walkers scrape up and down hallways, a couple of wheelchairs roll around. Mostly we do what we've always done, we just do it slower.

The disgustingly effervescent voice grated on the intercom that piped announcements into all the apartments at the Village. The blasted thing interrupted my afternoon reading of the latest nursery rhyme mystery, "Death Goes 'Round the Mulberry Bush".

"Everyone come to the dining area at two o'clock for Bingo. And, in honor of President's Day," the voice continued, "refreshments of cherry cobbler a la mode, with slivers of chocolate bark will be served, thanks to Garcon'." There was a barely audible giggle at the pronouncement of the name.

The chef's name was Rick Garrison, but Annie, our new director of coercion—sorry, recreation—seemed to be sweet on him. She insisted on calling him Garcon', hoping, I supposed, to score some points with him.

Rick was also new to the place although, for me at least, he was a welcome addition. He was a big burly stevedore-looking guy; dark hair, Mediterranean complexion and cold dark eyes that never held a hint of laughter. But the man could cook! Meals had become inventive and enjoyable since he showed up. The desserts, especially, were, as my granddaughter would say, "to die for!" And I should know, I am somewhat of a dessert connoisseur.

As I returned from my sweets-induced reverie I heard an insistent, familiar knock at my door. Why Maggie Taylor rapped out the beat to 'shave and a haircut' was beyond me, but it had been her calling card since I had moved into the gloriously depressing Golden Harvest. The incessant knocking continued as I lumbered to the door and opened it to Maggie's expertly made-up face and immaculately coiffed hair. I managed an almost smile between chubby cheeks and gritted teeth as I held the door for her. "Why, hello, Maggie. What a pleasant surprise!" She was dressed in dark blue slacks and a blue floral-print blouse. I blinked at the ensemble. "Are you blue today?" I quipped.

"Ha ha," she said and twirled in my doorway for effect. "Do you like my new outfit?"

"Well," I drawled, "the pattern of that blouse looks like blue flowers growing up your neck and into those curls in your blue hair. Come to think of it though, it does make you look a bit taller."

Maggie stood a petite five foot two with the proverbial eyes of blue, and the years had been kind to her. She had managed to maintain her youthful weight and fretted when it ballooned above one hundred fifteen.

"I've put on a few pounds and had to pick up some new clothes. It was easier than taking off the weight."

"Oh, boo hoo. I'd like to weigh in as light as you."

I'm five foot ten and tip the scales at a healthy two hundred forty-five—that's after I deduct the allowable fifteen pounds for my clothing. I couldn't really sympathize with her dilemma. I don't think I had weighed one-fifteen since grade school.

"Oh Helen, I didn't mean anything by that. You're fine just the way you are."

Whenever I complained about my weight, Maggie's comment was the same as my mother's had always been, "Helen, you are just big-boned."

"Right. I am also big-skinned to cover the big bones."

"Don't be such a sourpuss. Come on down and play Bingo with us."

I placed my hands on my ample hips. "You know I don't play Bingo. Didn't like it when I had decent eyesight, and like it even less now that recognizing anything less pronounced than your blue hair is problematic."

Maggie placed her hands on her slight hips to match my confrontational stance. "Helen, you are not in that bad a shape. My goodness, you make yourself sound like a decrepit old fogey."

"Humph," I said, "isn't that what places like this are designed for?" I waved my arms around the room for effect.

"I don't know about you," she replied, "but I'm neither decrepit nor an old fogey. It's a case of mind over matter; you know that as well as anyone. Personally, I like to think I'm just now entering middle age."

"So," I smiled wickedly at her, "you figure you're going to be here playing Bingo until you're a hundred and forty or so?"

"That would be fine with me, as long as I still have my health."

She continued, that non-erasable smile lighting up her face. "At least come have cherry cobbler. Annie's Garcon' went to a lot of extra trouble for Presidents Day."

"Oh, alright; but it will interfere with my before dinner nap," I groused. "Let me freshen up."

She smiled at her conquest. "Is that a new pantsuit? It's very," she paused for the right word, "bright," she finally managed.

"You're the one who keeps telling me I'm too drab," I argued, "so I bought something with flowers." I attempted a pirouette to show off the full effect of my new blooms.

"Yes," she cocked her head and peeked at my backside as I twisted convulsively, "that does look like a bright pink hibiscus waving back there. I'm impressed that you're taking fashion advice from me."

I waved one hand in her direction as I checked the mirror and ran the fingers of my free hand through my short-cropped white hair. "Don't flatter yourself. I found it at Nifty Thrifty's 'Everything-you-can-stuff-in-a-bag-for-a-buck' sale." I knew that would get her.

"By the way," I added as I locked my door behind me, "you have lipstick on your teeth."

Maggie snapped her lips closed.

One for me!

She stopped at one of the padded benches that lined the halls, pulled a mirror and a tissue from her purse and wiped the color from her teeth.

Chapter 5

Just Maggie n' Me

Maggie and I were friends long before the Golden Harvest. We grew up together, made mud pies from the same puddle. I can't remember a time we hadn't depended on each other. As we walked down the hall that day for our cherry cobbler, she hooked her arm through mine, throwing us a little off balance; at least she didn't insist on skipping like we were back in grade school. We followed Elsie Barstow, "of the New Hampshire Barstow's", as she constantly reminded all within earshot. She was dressed in a peach flowered housedress haphazardly buttoned, and stepped, not so lightly but definitely fantastically, in bright orange slippers. Her outfit totally clashed with my bright pink hibiscus number.

"I wonder what the New Hampshire Barstow's would think of Miss Elsie's getup?" I whispered to Maggie.

"Shh," warned Maggie, also in a whisper. "She'll hear you."

Elsie turned and shook an arthritic finger at Maggie. "I hear you talking about me, Maggie Taylor. Shame on you." Elsie was a retired schoolteacher, thus the churlish reprimand.

I smiled innocently at Maggie.

"Actually, Elsie," Maggie lied through her sparkly clean teeth, "I was just commenting to Helen about your slippers. Are they Comfort Zones?"

"Why, yes they are."

"I thought so. I've always wanted a pair, but they're a little pricey for my pocket book."

"I always say you get what you pay for. Comfort Zones are the best slippers on the market for these old feet. Why, my bunions don't hurt a bit when I'm wearing these." With that, she plopped down in the nearest chair, lifted her feet in the air, admired her orange slippers and rubbed those pesky bunions.

Ah, yes. We do get intimate details from some of our residents about their ailments, something else in which I have absolutely no interest. I sat down and stared across the dining room while Maggie sympathized and gave Elsie advice on caring for, or curing, her bunions. *Please, Lord,* I prayed to myself, *bring on the cobbler and save me from joining this conversation.*

"isn't that right, Helen?"

"What?" I jumped at the sound of my name.

"I was telling Elsie you and I have known each other forever."

"Yes, yes, that's right—forever." I stretched to look in the direction of the kitchen. "Where's that cobbler?"

Maggie turned to Elsie. "Helen's a little out of sorts today."

Elsie smiled and nodded sympathetically. "Have some of that high fiber cereal for breakfast tomorrow. It works wonders for me." She pointed that bony finger in my direction. "And some stewed prunes; have the cook warm them; that will do the trick."

I scowled at Maggie. She grinned back through those sparkling teeth.

One for Maggie!

"Helen went off to college after high school, but we always kept in touch."

Elsie nodded. "What did you study, Helen? I've always been glad I got my teaching degree."

Before I could say something incriminating about know-it-all kids being pretty much unteachable, Maggie cut in—again. "Helen earned a major in business and a minor in journalism."

"Journalism," Elsie harrumphed. "What about you, Maggie? Didn't you go to college?"

Maggie faltered. She didn't like to talk about what might have been missed opportunities.

To fill in the silence and curtail Elsie's staring, I spoke up. "No, she stayed home to work as a receptionist in her father's plant, and help take care of her mother." For me, that was quite a conversation.

Elsie gave Maggie her 'Poor You' look.

"It all worked out for the best. I met Bill while I worked there. He came to make a sales call on my father, and said he fell in love with me at first sight. We were married the following spring. Helen came home to be my maid of honor."

"How romantic," Elsie sighed.

"You're sitting in my chair." The voice from behind me was frail but determined. I turned to look when the voice became a physical annoyance that latched onto my shoulder. One of the aides took the intruder's arm. "Now, Miss Ora, it's not dinner time. We can sit anywhere for snacks. Come sit over here with Henry."

"I don't like Henry," she shouted. "He picks his nose when he eats."

"Would you like to sit with Eleanor and Hazel?" She led the

pouting Ora to another table. Were I a better person, I would have felt guilty for not giving up my seat.

I turned back to the sweetly sickening romantic conversation that continued between my dessert mates.

"What colors did you have in your wedding, Maggie, dear?"

Maggie looked at me and gave me a "You-keep-your-mouth-shut-Helen" look. That look, as scary as her Bill might have thought it was, had never frightened me.

"Maggie's colors were lime green and burnt orange. Imagine me, just a few pounds lighter than now, in lime green and orange. I vaguely resembled a giant bowl of sherbet." I shuddered at the recollection. "Not a pleasant sight."

Maggie's eyes went all misty and her chin quivered. "The colors were lovely, very springy. I'm sorry you were uncomfortable in the dress. I thought you looked beautiful."

"It was your wedding day! You thought the whole world was beautiful! The flowers were beautiful. The rain was beautiful! Even the washed-out roads after that torrential downpour were beautiful!"

I was pushing her too far. This is where I usually get into trouble. I decided to back off—not my usual style. I leaned forward and patted her arm. "And rightfully so. It was your special day. So I looked like something you had floating around in the wedding punch. It wasn't about me; it was about you. And you were a beautiful bride."

She sniffled. "Thanks, Helen."

"I still hated that dress," I muttered. Then I smiled in her direction.

"I know." She smiled back and all was right with us again.

"You looked delicious, though." I looked at her and we started giggling; we had to hold onto each other to keep from falling off our chairs with the laughter that followed. Elsie eyed us with quiet disdain before moving to sit with Miss Ora and Eleanor.

Chapter 6

Hi, Ho, Hi, Ho,
It's back to work I Go

After our cheery cherry repast, I excused myself lest I get caught up in the Bingo frenzy. Cards had been passed out; I slid mine toward Maggie and headed back to the quiet of my room. Even from down the hall I could hear Annie holler, "B-2" loud enough for Beelzebub to hear, in case he'd snagged one of the cards.

As I scampered, senior-citizen-style, toward my room I thought about my good friend, the pleasantly irritating Maggie. Growing up we were the Yin and Yang of adolescents. She was courteous, I a curmudgeon; she soft and frilly, I soiled and frumpy. We were a testament to the adage that opposites attract. Through seventy years of mud pies, puppy love and lost loves, we have remained as close as two opposite pole magnets, sucked together by some force of nature neither of us cares to break—the sherbet bridesmaid dress notwithstanding.

When her Bill died of a sudden heart attack shortly after their 47th wedding anniversary, Maggie took it all in stride with her usual composure—at least on the surface. I stayed by her side those six months when she cried herself to sleep every night. I felt so helpless. And I was angry with Bill for deserting her like that. Then one day she woke up, and as we were having breakfast said, "Helen, I've moped long enough. I'm going to sell this big old rambling place and move into that new retirement village."

"What?" I gasped. "With all those OLD FOLKS?"

She patted my liver-spotted hand across the table. "In case you haven't noticed, Helen, we *are* those old folks."

She finished breakfast, dressed in her navy blue suit with white polka dots, and went to talk to a realtor to make the arrangements. She seemed happy with her decision and never looked back.

Personally, I'm still mad at Bill. I had gone to stay with her for that period, knowing I could help her through her loss. I had suffered through the loss of my own husband, Harry, fifteen years earlier. Harry's heart attack, however, had been a twenty-something big-busted bimbo named Chloe, for whom he divorced me. I have come to the conclusion that the separation issues caused by divorce are worse than death because, unless the ex-moves to Australia, you are forced to view the body for the rest of your natural life.

Okay, so maybe I wasn't mad at Bill—maybe it was Harry's departure that still stirred me up. I was probably getting my hackles up right now thinking about him, but I couldn't be sure, as I didn't know exactly where my hackles might be.

I awoke from my mental wanderings and realized I had passed the door to my apartment. I cursed Harry under my breath as I turned and marched back to my door, unlocked it and let myself in. I wasn't about to share this information with Maggie. She has tried for years to force me to face my "Harry issues", as she calls them. I don't have any issues—at least none that sticking a stake through his fat, flatulent body and into his cold heart wouldn't cure.

I plopped down at my desk and tried to do some writing. On the wall in front of me hung a mirror; I looked up and was startled by my reflection. Ellyn thinks mirrors make a room seem larger, bless her heart. I looked at my sagging face in that reflective glass. I don't allow myself too many sobering thoughts, it's too darned depressing. I look around this place at all these folks in various stages of aging, and I'm reminded of a time when old people irritated me. Now when I squint into a mirror, one of those old fogies squints back, taunting me; her thinning snow-white hair needs a perm and her wrinkled, age-blotched face resembles a dingy blouse that wasn't removed promptly from the dryer.

Today I stared at that face and wondered whether to run it through touch-up cycle in the dryer or take the steam iron to it. I checked once, but there's no selection on my iron marked 'skin'. So you see why I steer away from serious thinking—at least on a personal level. I'm certainly not against writing about other people's foibles.

Which reminded me, I'd have to ask Maggie at dinner if she knew anything about the new resident who just moved into apartment 110. I still had a paper to put out, and if Maggie didn't know about this new character, my other source, Sophia, would. Not much gets by those two.

Chapter 7

You'll Lift Off Soon, Lennie Moon

*G*olden Harvest is laid out like a big square open in the middle. That way, all apartments, inside and outside, have access to the outdoors and a small patio. Inside, a wide hallway provides access to the apartments on both sides. The rooms on the outside wall open to their little patios and a sidewalk around the entire building. It's wide enough to accommodate wheelchairs, and sports a railing to steady anyone who has the urge to walk to no place in particular for no apparent reason.

A six-foot high brick wall runs across the front and down both sides of the property to protect us from marauding yuppies. The gated entrance remains locked, with access only by those who can remember the code. It's supposedly a security feature; I'm not sure if it's to secure us from the public at large or them from us. A thick grove of loblolly pines secures the back of the property from any other intruders. George Hardestee, Golden Harvest's administrator, lives in a small cottage beyond the loblolly forest.

The inside apartments open to their patios and an enclosed central garden adorned with patches of flowers, shrubs and withering potted plants. There is also a sidewalk, a shortcut through this enclosed area from the east wing to the west wing—or north to south—I never have been good at directions, giving or taking.

My apartment opens to the central garden, and as I looked out my window that day I could see two people puttering around out there. Lennie Moon, part-time groundskeeper and maintenance worker, full-time UFO enthusiast, concentrated on his hedge trimming. He stood up, ball cap tilted sideways on his head, orange-red hair spewing out underneath like an oversized, rusty scouring pad. He stretched and gazed into the sky. Lennie was medium height, medium build, and of indeterminate age. I would guess he was probably in his late twenties. He was not bad looking, just mostly forgettable, one of those people who can be almost invisible in a crowd. I once considered introducing him to my granddaughter, Ellyn, but the thought of progeny from that coupling was a scary prospect. Over-achieving computer nerd meets space cadet; it would never work. She would be eternally bored, Lennie eternally confused. Their kids might discover ways to computer-generate themselves to distant planets but, once there, would disappear into universal oblivion.

I watched him at his work, completely engrossed in the task at hand. Lennie did have a nice smile, but you can't build a relationship on pleasant facial features. His skin glistened tan and leathery from working in the sun, and his loose fitting, grimy T-shirt read "Property of Area 51". He dropped back down on his knees and continued the tedious pruning, snipping at the hedge ahead of him with what looked like a pair of kitchen shears. He placed the clippings in a bucket to his left, perusing each twig with dark brown eyes that only sparked with life when he cornered someone to discuss gardening or UFO's.

His mind was filled with theories and trivia about our government's cover-up of alien invasions. When allowed to discuss his ideas, his eyes burned bright and he became very articulate, but if asked a simple question that required a personal response he could only mumble an answer. Lennie was harmless, if single-minded, and I sort of liked the kid. He had conviction, and he didn't go out of his way to make people like him—kind of an idiot-savant version of me.

The other person in the garden was my second source, after Maggie, for information. I decided now was as good a time as any to interrogate her about our newest resident. I slipped into a sweater, grabbed my yellow legal pad, and stepped out the door.

Lennie waved in my direction. "Hey, Mrs. P. How's it goin'?"

I returned the wave. "Hi, Lennie. Seen any UFO's lately?"

He pulled himself to his feet and ambled over to where I stood. "As a matter of fact, I've been getting some strange vibes from this place lately. I think there's something funny going on around here."

"Oh, really?" I humored him. "Like what? Do you suspect an alien invasion of the old folk's home?"

He shook his head. "I'm not sure what it is, but something strange is happening. I've been feeling weird electrical impulses in certain places." He leaned forward and whispered, "The vibration is really strong around the administration office and Miss James recreation room. I'd stay away from there, if I were you."

I patted his shoulder. "Gotcha, Lennie. Thanks for the warning, I'll stay away; not that I need any excuse for avoiding the recreation around here."

Lennie nodded. "Uh, okay."

The jolts were probably static electricity from him schlepping down the carpeted hallway in his steel-toed sneakers, but I wasn't going to burst his alien bubble. He exited the garden with another wave and a further reminder for me to keep my eyes open.

Chapter 8

The Pixie on the Patio

I walked over to where my informant stood. She stared at the parched dirt around her small cement square of patio, hands on hips, clicking her tongue and talking to no one—at least no one I could see—about the deplorable state of the garden. She pointed with pruning shears to a spot in front of her. "This garden needs some bone meal or coffee grounds to aerate the soil. It really works."

If you spent enough time around her, you could almost believe Sophia Gardenelli communicated with beings not seen by us 'common folk'. But then Sophia, herself, didn't look like us common folk. At four-foot-six she resembled a garden gnome, or a wizened little leprechaun or pixie.

She dressed in bright gauzy garments with permanent wrinkles, the skirts flowed to the ground and gave the illusion she was floating everywhere she traveled. I've watched her, and I couldn't swear she wasn't. Her hair, white as the sparkle of a model's smile, save for one glossy black streak on the right side, fell in clusters fine as spider webs to her shoulders. Today the webs were held in place by a royal purple silk scarf that

31

hung nearly to her skirt hem.

I peeked over her shoulder, thinking I might catch a glimpse of her conversation companion. Seeing nothing or no one else in the vicinity, I cleared my throat and asked, "So, what's the scoop on 110?"

She turned to me as though she knew all along I was there, and raised her head to look into my eyes. "Her name is LeeAnne—all one word, but with both the L and the A capitalized—Warner." She pointed the shears in my direction and added, "And that red hair came out of a bottle."

"That goes without saying. Nobody, especially nobody our age, has hair that color."

"Oh, but she did at one time—natural redhead. Yes, it was exactly that color when she was younger."

"You knew her, then, when she was young?"

"I have my sources."

I rubbed my hands together in anticipation. "I know. So, tell me; I want to know all the good stuff. And speaking of stuff, she sure did bring a lot to put in her little apartment." I made myself as comfortable as possible on the cement bench.

"Actually," Sophia said, "when she moved here to Golden Harvest she left most of it behind, except for lots of memories and a few baubles."

She stage-whispered into my left ear, "Over the years LeeAnne had many loves, none of them long-lasting. Some attempted to hold her interest, but she was a fickle lover and tended to change allegiances as often as farmers change overalls—about once a week, on Saturday." She cocked her head and one side of her mouth curved into a smile at her little joke.

My eyes widened; she patted my arm, but said no more. I could hardly contain myself, and her silence was irritating. This was better than I could have imagined. I placed my legal pad on my lap. "Was she ever married?"

"Oh yes. She married Charles Warner in '51. Her maiden name was Shaw."

This was too good! I jotted down the name and date. "What did he think of her involvements?"

"For years Charlie indulged LeeAnne's fickle heart, until he dropped dead one Sunday while putting the final touches on a sauna for her latest love."

I gasped, Sophia grinned.

"Stoke and Smoulder's Crematorium—I think their slogan is 'We Burnum and Returnum', furnished a lovely Chinese style urn for his ashes."

I couldn't stifle my laugh. "You made that up!"

Sophia shrugged and continued as if I hadn't spoken. "She debated about where to display it—should it be with the pottery she loved in '82," she pointed her shears to the left, "or with her Chinese period pieces from '79?" She put index finger to chin, "Or was it '78?" She slapped her hands against her frothy skirt. "No matter. LeeAnne finally decided to place him in the room with her latest, and last, great love."

It was my turn to click my tongue.

She patted my shoulder. "Yes, Charlie came to temporary/permanent rest in the hot house sauna with her orchids. The Chinese urn and Charlie—or what remains of him—came with her to Golden Harvest. The orchids, unfortunately, stayed behind."

"Orchids? Her last great love was *orchids*? Sophia, that's

terrible! You had me believing the woman was … was … well, you know what I was thinking! You're awful!" I hoisted myself up and turned to stomp away from Sophia and her invisible companion.

"Don't you want to know the rest of the story?" she teased.

I plopped back down on the bench. "Oh, all right, but just the facts." I shook my pen in her elfin face and sputtered, "No more double ent-entr-double meanings!"

"I was only attempting to furnish something juicy for your column—something more interesting than 'Jo Blow just blew in from Blowhard, after retiring from Blowhard's Bubbleblow factory.' Don't you ever get tired of that trash?"

I bit my tongue to keep from responding to her cutting remarks, especially since she had an uncanny way of knowing everything about everyone. My emotions were less important than getting the story; and, all in all, this sounded like a good one. I placed my hands in my lap, legal pad at the ready. "Go on."

She leaned forward and mouthed the words as if relaying some dark secret. With me sitting and her standing, we were about eye to eye. "LeeAnne was on the stage."

"An actress?" I nearly shouted. "On Broadway?"

She raised her hands and slapped at the air. "Keep your voice down, will you? This whole place has ears, no matter how deaf some of these old geezers try to make you think they are."

"Well, was she?" I tried to keep my excitement to a minimum, but could barely contain myself. I had never met a real actress, unless you counted Janine Hopgood who, in seventh grade, had played the Snow Queen in our class production of 'The Snow Queen Saves Christmas'. Janine never let us forget her command performance, even now, here at Golden Harvest. She cornered all the 'newbies' and bored them with her story—unless someone got to them first and gave them fair warning.

Sophia tapped my shoulder and broke into my wandering thoughts. "Where were you just then? Looked like you'd slipped off to LaLa Land. Thought I was going to have to get the orderlies out here to escort you to the padded room. Do you want to hear about LeeAnne or not?"

I heaved a sigh. "Yes, of course. Go on."

She sat beside me on the bench and attempted to brush her skirt smooth with her hands. "To answer your question, no, she wasn't exactly on Broadway. But she was very well known in her time."

"I've never heard of anyone by the name of LeeAnne anything who was famous. What did she do?"

"She didn't use her given name, silly." She leaned closer, conspiratorially. "She was a fan dancer," she whispered.

"What? You mean like Isadora What's-her-name?"

"Shhh!" She waved her hands up and down like a large moth. "Yes, exactly like Isadora What's-her-name."

"Scandalous! Wait until I write this up in the newsletter!" I added that information to my notes.

She stood, all four-and-a-half feet of her, and put hands on tiny hips. "You can't write *that* up in the newsletter, Helen."

"Why not? You certainly didn't say it was off the record! I have a job to do. How else will the residents get to know all the newcomers who show up at this place? I have an obligation to my readers!"

"Readers!" harrumphed Sophie. "A bunch of nosy old people who have nothing better to do. Helen, sometimes you take your 'job' almost as seriously as Janine Hopgood does her Snow Queen career."

I jumped up from the bench—as much of a jump as a septuagenarian can manage. I refused to stay in the presence of someone who put me in the same category as the Snow Queen.

"That was uncalled for, Sophia. And why can't I write about her career?"

"Let's just say, I don't think it is something she would want people to know. Fan dancing is not quite a—how should I say it?—legitimate form of the arts." She wrinkled her nose. "Rather burlesque and bawdy, actually. How would you feel if it were you and people were made aware that you gyrated around on stage and allowed cigar-smoking gentlemen to pull feathers from your fan, or scarves from your," she stumbled a little here, "from your—whatever!" She fluttered her arms in the air again for effect.

I grabbed one of her wrists in flight. "Sophia, if you don't stop that arm-waving, one of these days you're going to fly right out of here."

She stopped flailing and I continued. "I think this LeeAnne's career would be of great interest to my reading public. Why would she mind?"

She shrugged. "You could ask her, but then she would want to know where you got the information she's tried so desperately to hide all these years." She glided toward her apartment, then turned and flashed me a sly 'I-dare-you' smile.

"It's up to you, of course. Just leave me out of it. She might not get too angry that you asked." With that she floated through the door and disappeared into her secret elfin sanctuary.

As I stood up and pondered how best to approach Ms.

LeeAnne Warner about her career on the stage, Wally Cox tentatively poked his head out the door of his apartment. He grinned and waved to me. He was a reincarnation of the late actor, Wally Cox, who played on that Mr. Peepers show. His name was actually Bernie Cox, but everyone here at Golden Harvest called Him Wally, and it stuck. Some called him Mr. Peepers behind his back. I could relate. Because of my size, I had been subjected to some of those same kinds of slurs, and knew they could really hurt. Our Wally, however, seemed oblivious to them—or maybe, because he was so short, they went way over his head.

He stood about five-foot-seven, his dark blue eyes magnified to saucer-size behind horn-rimmed glasses. No matter what time of day or what the weather, he always dressed in a suit complete with dress shirt, jacket and oversized bow tie. Not one of those clip-on things, either—a real honest-to-goodness around-the-neck bow tie. Today was no exception. The suit was dark, the shirt powder blue and the tie black with blue ducks, or some species of flying creature.

Lately he had been popping up around me like a myopic jack-in-the-box, wearing that goofy grin and stammering greetings. When he approached me today, those magnified eyeballs were in a direct line with my chest. He quickly averted them and squeaked a nearly inaudible, "Hello."

I didn't think he was intentionally leering, but our height difference put him at a distinct disadvantage. It was disconcerting though, especially since Maggie had noticed him following me around, and teased me about my new admirer.

I flashed him an indulgent smile and escaped back into my apartment. Even if he'd been soaking wet in that suit, he would have probably tipped the scales at no more than one-forty-five, so I outweighed him by a hundred pounds. I wasn't afraid of him; I knew I could sit on him and incapacitate him for the rest of his natural life. But the whole stalker/admirer thing was getting a bit creepy.

Chapter 9

Oh, Dear, What Can the Matter Be?
Someone's Replaced Dear George Hardestee

In all the excitement of the news about LeeAnne Warner, I was late getting to dinner; the salads and tea had already been set on our table when I joined Maggie. She wore a tired, glum look, kind of blue to match her hair. I could hardly wait to fill her in on my conversation with Sophia. "You'll never guess what I just heard about the new resident!"

Then I took a second look at her downcast expression. "What's wrong?" I asked. "You look like you've lost your best friend," I spread my arms wide, "but here I am!"

She humored me with a rather wan smile and a deep, mournful sigh.

"What?" I asked again. "Did you lose big-time at Bingo?"

She leaned closer and, almost in a whisper, said, "You mustn't repeat a word of this."

Oh, oh. My ears pricked up. Never say those words to a journalist.

Maggie caught the hungry look. "I mean it! Promise me, Helen. You can't tell anyone. If you don't promise, I'm not telling you a thing."

Exasperated, I agreed. "Okay. What is it?"

"Pinky swear," she said, holding up her right hand, pinky curled toward me.

"Geez, Maggie, what are we, grade-schoolers?"

She frowned, the furrows in her forehead deep enough to plant potatoes.

"All right, pinky swear," I said, hooking little fingers with her.

Just then the aide/waitress stopped by our table to inquire about our salad dressing choices. Maggie pulled her hand back. "Of course I'll come to your room for a game of Gin Rummy after dinner, Helen. You don't have to make a big deal out of it."

I had to munch my way through the whole meal, including dessert, with Maggie silent as a mime, but without the interesting hand gestures. All the while, Maggie tested my appetite with her sighs and depressed looks, merely picking at her food.

I managed to finish my dessert of chocolate pudding cake. It's one of my favorites, but I was so irritated by Maggie's gloomy attitude, the joy of savoring its moist goodness was nearly lost.

However, it didn't stop me from pointing to hers and asking, rather curtly, "Are you going to eat that?"

She shoved it across the table to me. I cleaned the plate and rose to leave. "So I'll see you later?" I questioned my mute dinner partner.

She nodded, still impersonating some voiceless character. I shook my head, more than a little curious about her strange behavior, and ambled on home.

I pulled out my legal pad and transferred all the information I could remember about my earlier conversation with Sophia about Mrs. LeeAnne Warner. A light tapping emanated from the hallway; a cane-wielding resident making his or her way home, I assumed. I kept an ear open for Maggie's signature knock, although I was still a little miffed with her for the silent treatment at the dinner table. My revelation about apartment 110 was so good I wanted to share it with her. I tapped my pen on my tablet, in cadence with the rapping outside my door, while I played over in my mind Maggie's secretive behavior. She had acted like a scared witness in a very bad spy movie.

The infernal noise in the hallway now included an agitated voice. I peeked through my security peephole to pinpoint the disturbance. There stood Maggie, head and frown larger than life through that little hole; her eyes stared back at me, still looking angry or afraid, it was hard to tell. Probably angry, the way she shoved past me into the room when I opened the door. "Why didn't you answer the door when I knocked?"

"Excuse me, but I didn't recognize that as your knock. What happened to 'shave and a haircut'?" I tapped out the 'two bits' rhythm on the inside of the door as I closed it.

She turned, tears in her blue eyes, grabbed my arm, pulled me toward the small sofa—more correctly a loveseat, however incongruous that seems at my age—and sagged down on one end. "Quit playing games, Helen. This is serious."

I sat down beside her, an intimacy I'd shared with few people, and none had been on this particular piece of furniture. "Okay, okay. What's up? Are we being invaded by aliens?"

At that Maggie burst into full-fledged blubbering. "Evritigis ajo q u!" she sobbed, which I translated as best I could to, "Everything's a joke to you."

I must have been close because when I murmured, "I'm not joking, I'm just trying to figure out what has you so upset," and patted her shoulder, she calmed down a bit. I handed her a box of tissues, she scooped up several and snuffed into them. I didn't know what else to do, nurturing is not one of my strong points. I retrieved a damp cloth from the bathroom for her and sat back down in silence while she swiped it across her face and attempted to compose herself.

She placed her hands, still clutching the damp cloth, into her lap, sighed deeply and stared somewhere into space. Had it been Lennie, I wouldn't have worried about the spacey stare, but this was my friend. Maggie looked a sight. I'd not seen her this visibly upset since Bill died. I pulled the cloth from her grasp and tossed it across the room toward the kitchen counter; it missed and fell to the tile floor in a soggy heap. I took Maggie's icy cold hand in mine. Her face was blotchy from crying and her blue flowered outfit, that had bloomed so fresh and crisp earlier in the day, now hung on her frame like wilted foliage.

"George is being replaced," she blurted out.

"George Hardestee, our administrator?"

She nodded, a fresh flow of tears ready to tumble down her cheeks at any moment. I absent-mindedly handed her the box of tissues again.

George Hardestee was our long-time friend and, although a couple of years younger than Maggie and me, was pushing hard against the age of retirement. He was sixty-seven and had been a widower for many years. When his wife, Gwen, died of cancer after twenty years together, he threw himself completely into his accounting business. He said his work consoled him; when nothing else made sense, numbers brought balance back into his life. He and Gwen had no children. After her death George had only his business and a few close friends; Maggie and I counted ourselves among his closest. For a while we tried to fix him up with some of our widowed friends, until he begged us to please stop, he liked his life just the way it was.

He would have been a good catch, though. He was steady and secure, honest to a fault, not bad looking although, at five-foot-eight, a bit short. But, then, I gauge everything from my elevated five-foot-ten perspective. For someone say, Maggie's size, he was a perfectly presentable height. His full head of hair had gone snow-white in his forties, giving him a distinguished appearance. Lately he had become what some people describe as portly. Over the years he had escorted me to many functions, some at his invitation, some at mine. He was, indeed, a dear friend.

I smiled. "Did he finally decide to join the ranks of us seniors?"

"It was not by choice," she sniffed. "He's being investigated for some kind of financial mismanagement."

"What?" I shouted. George had been a CPA and financial manager for over forty years; in fact, we all became acquainted when he first went into business. As a financial planner he had handled stock portfolios for me as well as Bill and Maggie. I believed in George; he wouldn't mishandle anyone's money. When he retired from regular practice, he sat on the board for this place and was elected administrator before either Maggie or I moved in.

"Where did you hear such nonsense?"

"It's not nonsense, and I heard it from George. I had been hearing rumors ever since that couple came in about a month ago and ran that so-called audit. Do you remember that?"

I absent-mindedly scratched my head with my pen. "Yes, weren't their names Jamie and Frankie? I never figured out which was which."

"That was them. Jamie was the guy, Frankie, his wife—or so they said. I didn't trust her, she had shifty eyes—wouldn't look at you when she talked. Always had her sights on something over your shoulder, or was checking out what Jamie was doing." She shook a finger in my direction, "Never trust a person with shifty eyes, Bill always said, they are up to no good."

"What prompted the audit?" I asked, in an attempt to get her back on track.

George said they approached the board and had some authority through the state to check senior living centers. Now they've come up with what they claim is proof of some bogus payouts. As of tomorrow, Frankie and Jamie Cunningham are the temporary administrators, and George is out until this mess is cleared up."

I stood up and began to pace the small apartment. "Can they do that? What's George going to do? He sold his house and built that little cabin behind the retirement home. He practically lives here!"

"He's going to stay with his sister temporarily. The board offered to let him rent one of the apartments here, but he felt it would be easier for everyone if he made himself scarce for a while."

I couldn't stop pacing. "But doesn't that make him look guilty? Shouldn't he stay here and fight the allegations? He could stay in his cabin. He built that with his own money."

"That thieving couple took it over. The cabin is one of the things those two questioned—they posed the possibility that some of the materials were paid for with Golden Harvest funds."

"That's ridiculous! George wouldn't take a cent that didn't belong to him."

Maggie latched onto my hand as I stomped past her. "You and

I know that, but the board doesn't. We've got to hope the board figures it out."

I turned and grabbed her by the shoulders. "We can't leave it to them; there's not a person left on that board who can muster up a conscious thought of his own. They're like a bunch of lemmings. If one of them votes to oust George, the rest will follow suit; but it won't be them jumping off the cliff, it will be them throwing George off. We've got to find out what's really going on!"

Maggie jumped up and gave me a hug. "I was hoping you would say that!"

We sat back on the tiny sofa. I grabbed my yellow legal pad and wrote at the top of the next clean page in bold letters: PROJECT GEORGE, and under that: Number 1. *Find out who Frankie and Jamie Cunningham really are.* We stared at the yellow pad; I wondered how we were going to accomplish that first act. And I wasn't sure what Number 2 would be. I was sure the Cunninghams were up to something. But figuring out their evil plan might require incorporating some spying skills I had only engaged in vicariously through the mystery novels I enjoyed reading.

Maggie, fully aware of my jump-into-everything-head-first way of solving problems, grabbed the legal pad from my hands. "Helen, please get that look off your face. We are not going to do anything dangerous," she slammed the pad down on the table, "or borderline illegal."

I picked my pad back up and held it to my chest. "How dangerous can it possibly be? We live in an old folk's home, for crying out loud."

"I wish you wouldn't call it that, Helen. You make it sound as though we are a bunch of doddering old fools, and I, for one, am not doddering or a fool."

"Okay, I apologize."

To get her back in focus, I mentioned my conversation with Lennie about something strange going on around the office. "Considering what you just told me, maybe he's on to something."

She managed a condescending smile and shook her head. "Lennie is a harmless, if misguided, individual," she said.

I had to agree; still, I wondered if Lennie might just be picking up vibes that weren't as alien as they at first seemed.

Chapter 10

You Tell Me Your Secrets
I'll Tell You Mine

We sat there for a while, each of us engrossed in our own thoughts. Maggie stared at her clasped hands, I stared at the words on my legal pad, and doodled squiggles and question marks in the margins.

Maggie finally broke the silence. "So what was the news you were so desperate to share at the dinner table?"

In the light of her news about George, I was a bit embarrassed; mine sounded like cheap gossip. But the guilt didn't slow me down for long.

"Sophia told me..."

Maggie raised her eyebrows and let out an exasperated snort. "Sophia, huh? That woman has her nose in everybody's business!"

I bit my tongue lest I let slip the fact that she and Sophia ran a very close race in that department. After all, the two of them were my best sources of information; I didn't want to burn any bridges. I held up my hands, "Just let me finish. I would have asked you first about the new resident, but I happened to see Sophia in the garden this afternoon."

"Which new resident? 110 or 122?" Maggie half turned so she could catch my startled look.

"110. Who's in 122?"

A slow, satisfied smile came to play on her lips. "Elsworth Lumley. Do you have any more of that nice chamomile tea? I could use a cup." She got up, crossed to open the cupboard over the sink and fiddled around filling my electric teakettle. "Would you like a cup?"

"I don't care. Sure. Who's Elswood Lumble? And when did he show up?" I hoisted myself off the sofa and followed her to the kitchenette.

She dropped tea bags in the cups. "It's *Elsworth Lumley,* and he moved in today." She paused and stared into space. "But there's something not right—he doesn't look like he belongs here."

"Why?" I asked, as I dug around in the cupboard for some cookies. "What's wrong with him?" I had visions of some poor soul in need of around the clock nursing care or maybe in an iron lung or something. "And how did I miss him?"

"Well, if you would socialize a little more you'd know these things."

I threw my arms in the air. "That's what I've got you for."

The compliment was lost on her. She turned to pour water from the whistling kettle into the cups. "Me and Sophia Gardenelli," she harrumphed.

So that was it. She intended to drag this out because I'd spoken to Sophia. "Okay," I conceded, "I'll tell you what I found out about 110 and you fill me in on 122."

Maggie mulled that over as she carried her tea and a couple

fig bars back to the sofa. "Alright," she finally said. She bit into one of the stale cookies, grimaced and pointed it at me like a weapon. "You first."

I sat down on the chair to her left and told her about LeeAnne and her glamorous, if somewhat dubious, past. For once, Maggie didn't interrupt my recitation. In fact, I could see her eyes widen in surprise; twice she actually licked her lips as she took in all this juicy stuff. I enjoyed my one-upmanship; I don't get ahead of Maggie very often in the 'Who's Who at the Harvest' gossip.

When I finally paused, she asked, "Did you see that diamond bracelet she wore to dinner last night?"

"Yeah, and the necklace too. I figured it was costume jewelry; who wears that much glitter to eat in our dining room?"

Maggie nodded. "Kind of what I thought. But what if it's real? An actress could have accumulated real jewels."

I nibbled a cookie and sipped my tea. "I suppose so. I guess if you've got it, you might as well flaunt it, as we used to say. Not that I ever had anything worth flaunting. We'll have to check out Mrs. Warner more thoroughly. I'll interview her for *The Harvester*; I've never interviewed a fan dancer before."

Maggie choked on her tea. "You've never even seen a fan dancer before, have you?"

I shook my head. "There's a first time for everything, they say." I pointed my half-eaten cookie in her direction. "Now it's your turn. Tell me about Mr. Lumley."

She leaned forward and let out a long breath. I hadn't heard Maggie sigh like that since we were kids. What in the world was going on here?

"I only caught a glimpse of him." Her face became animated,

just like when she told me about Billy Joe Halvert back in fourth grade. "But he's a hunk, as your granddaughter would say. Tall, looks like he must work out, carries himself well. He moved in with very few furnishings; a couple of chairs, a table, a bookcase and some boxes marked 'books'." She laughed, "Alma and Ruth fell all over themselves trying to get his attention, but he seems to be a man of few words. He merely nodded politely and smiled at them." She leaned back on the sofa, with that Billy Joe Halvert look still in her eyes. If I didn't watch her, she'd be in line with Ruth and Alma vying for Lumley's attention. I decided I had to find out about the new 'hunk' before the whole place went gaga.

We visited for a while, then Maggie said she'd better be going. "I'll see you for breakfast. Meanwhile, try to figure out how we are going to help George." She gave me a hug and scooted out the door.

I called George on his cell phone to check on him. He had settled into his sister's place and seemed to be doing fine. The Cunningham's showed no signs of going anywhere in the near future, so I relegated them to the back burner for now. I felt an urgent need to check out this Lumley character in whom Maggie had shown such interest. I didn't want her to get hurt by some gigolo.

I reread my notes. My journalistic juices began to flow in earnest. The Over-the-Hillton had gained some interesting characters, perhaps even some notoriety. The stories wouldn't hit the front page of the *Times*, but they might prove to be more exciting than what Sophia had referred to as the 'Joe Blow just retired from the Bubble blow Factory' pieces that she rudely said normally filled my newsletter.

I watched Mr. Lumley's movements for a couple of days to figure out his routine. Every morning he went to the workout room for an hour or more. There was nothing suspicious about that, except for the number of women who now made a point of exercising on a regular basis, too. I was determined to talk to him, but hadn't yet decided on a ploy; as I said, I have an aversion to all forms of physical fitness. Besides, there were too many other women to contend with in the workout room.

Lennie, the maintenance man/gardener, exited one of the apartments ahead of me on the day I finally decided to confront Mr. Lumley. Lennie's tool belt was strapped low around his waist, with a plunger thrown across his shoulder—Lennie, the plumbing soldier, off to battle the Nefarious Clogs. He nodded stiffly. "Morning, Mrs. P."

"Good morning, Lennie. How are you?"

His downcast eyes never looked up into mine. "Fine, fine," he said, and he hurried away. Odd behavior, even for someone as strange as Lennie.

I had decided to catch Elsworth Lumley in the hallway when he exited his room to go to lunch; I wanted to time it so I'd be outside his door and on my way to the dining room at the same time as he. As it turned out, I had to pace back and forth for a full five minutes, but managed to be in the right place, and headed in the right direction, when he opened his door.

He didn't look like an Elsworth or a Lumley. 6'2" at least, broad shoulders, slim waist, gray hair cut in a burr. Unlike the other men in our over-the-hill league he showed no signs of going soft; no sagging chin or muscles, no pudginess around the middle, not even a hint of a tremor as he reached out to firmly grasp the hand

I held out. "Helen Patterson," I said.

"Elsworth Lumley," he answered, disengaging his hand. His steel-gray eyes met my gaze and one side of his mouth curled up slightly into an almost-smile. I could feel my cheeks grow warm and I had to look away.

He was a statement in subtlety; sport shirt that matched his cold, gray eyes, open at the neck showing ample chest hair, salt and pepper gray like the short cropping on his head. His slacks were a darker charcoal gray. Except for his well-tanned skin, he might have stepped out of some old black-and-white movie.

Not that I was the least bit interested, but I checked his left hand for a wedding band. His ring finger showed no sign of having been banded recently. He'd moved in here alone, but the addition of a ring to his wardrobe might indicate he was still clinging to an absent spouse.

Having satisfied that aspect of my journalistic curiosity, I peered around him to try and get a peek into his apartment as he pulled the door closed. I caught sight of floor-to-ceiling bookcases on the back wall and a huge world map to the right, before the door clicked shut.

"Nice to have you here, Mr. Lumley." I smiled, I hoped innocently. "Lumley is an unusual name. Are you from around here?"

He returned the smile, also innocent, showing straight even teeth, somewhat yellowed, probably a former smoker. His deep baritone reply consisted of a simple, "No."

It would be difficult to get an interview if he continued to answer questions in monosyllables.

I continued my introduction. "I write a newsletter for the

residents here, and I like to include information about our newcomers." I found myself nearly running to keep up with his brisk, long-legged stride. "When would you be available for an interview? Nothing lengthy, just a few lines to help us all get better acquainted."

"I appreciate your interest Mrs. ..."

"Patterson," I said. "Helen Patterson."

"Ah, yes, Mrs. Patterson. I'm not much given to interviews. I'm a very private person."

I nodded. "I can appreciate that, Mr. Lumley. I don't intend to pry. My interview would only be a few words about you." I decided to hit him with my best punch. "The interview would answer some questions for our, shall I say, more curious, residents. If they don't read about you in the newsletter, I can assure you that you will be bombarded with the questions from now on."

He stopped abruptly and turned to me. "That sounds vaguely like a threat."

My hand involuntarily went to my chest and I gasped, "Oh dear me! I didn't intend to upset you. I would never threaten anyone. I only meant that some of the ladies here do tend to be a bit nosy."

The hooded gray eyes softened and he smiled. "I suppose you're right. Those women in the gym do hover around and attempt to engage me in conversation. Perhaps it would be better to assuage their curiosity."

I shook his hand again. "Thank you."

He returned my handshake and said, "I must applaud their dedication to keeping fit, though."

I had to laugh. "The fitness craze began with your appearance, I'm afraid."

He nodded as he resumed his determined stride toward the dining room. "Oh, I see." Without a break in forward motion, he cast those metallic eyes at me and asked, "So when would you like to conduct this interview?"

I had to look up to return his stare. "Any time that's convenient for you. I'd like to include it in this week's paper, if possible."

"I have some free time after lunch. If you would like to come by my apartment we could get the thing over with."

Not the most enthusiastic interviewee I'd tackled, but I agreed to meet him at one-thirty. As we walked down the hall side-by-side, Wally Cox strode by and glared at Mr. Lumley.

I nodded to him. "Hello, Wally."

"Helen." He returned my nod, but never took his eyes off Lumley as he passed us on the way to his usual table.

Chapter 11

Nothing is Black and White-
But Everything is Kind of Gray

At the door to the dining room Lumley made a sharp right to sit at a corner table alone; I couldn't help but notice he sat with his back to the wall, his gray eyes constantly checked out the entrance in true secret agent fashion. I joined Maggie at our usual table.

Annie's *Garcon'* had been attempting international cuisine, no doubt at Annie's insistence, and we were being subjected to a barrage of worldwide food and topics. Pictures of exotic people and places lined the walls; book reviews and sewing circles had been inundated with trivial information on such places as Greece, Sweden and China. According to the place cards at each table, the fare for this day was Mihshi Malfuf, and had its origin in Saudi Arabia. It appeared to be a mixture of ground beef and rice wrapped in cabbage leaves and boiled in some kind of tomato sauce. I poked at my cabbage wrap and rolled it around on my plate looking for an appropriate place to attack it. I finally managed to stab the cabbage log, and, without looking up said nonchalantly, "I have an appointment after lunch to interview your Mr. Lumley in 122."

Maggie, in her excitement, grabbed my arm as I hoisted a large forkful of food to my mouth. I lost the bite and was left with a huge tomato-red blotch on my shirtfront. She dipped her napkin into my ice water and scrubbed unsuccessfully on the stain. I whined that after lunch I was going to have to rush back to my room so I could change.

"Oh well, you needed to change anyway before seeing Mr. Lumley," she finally conceded.

I checked my attire. "Why? I looked presentable until you slopped mufli sushi all over me."

She rolled her eyes and shook her head. "It's Mihshi Malfuf. And I'd be willing to bet you pulled that get-up out of your ironing basket this morning."

I brushed my hands over my wrinkled lap. "Did not." Not exactly a fib. It had been draped over the ironing board and I'd decided it didn't look all that bad—but Miss Always-Washed-and-Pressed didn't need to be privy to that bit of information.

Maggie stood and took my arm. "Come on, let's go see if we can find you something decent to wear."

I pulled away. "Before dessert? Not on your life."

I don't think the cheesecake that was served was a traditional Saudi dish. No matter, it's another one of my favorites, and I made Maggie sit there, chin in hands, while I finished both mine and hers.

When I had daintily wiped my mouth she stood up again. "Can we go now?"

She dragged me back to my apartment and rummaged through my wardrobe, holding up various items before discarding them as unfit. I followed her around, picked up a not-too-wrinkled blouse that sort of matched my slacks and held it in front of me. She turned up her nose and shook her head.

I threw the blouse back into the ironing basket. "For crying out loud, Maggie, I'm not meeting the queen; it's an interview for a newsletter that few people care about and even fewer people read!"

She sighed as she chose a top she considered suitable and carried it to the ironing board. "Yes, but it's *Elsworth Lumley*."

I jammed the iron plug into the socket. "Maybe you should do the interview, then. At least you don't have tomato sauce on your shirt."

Maggie looked hurt as she licked her finger, checked the iron for sizzle and began pressing. "Now don't get testy, Helen, you don't mean that. You know I could never do as good a job with an interview as you. You're the writer."

I looked at her and grinned. "Yeah, but you're the one who thinks Mr. Lumley is a hunk."

She tossed the now wrinkle-free blouse across the ironing board. "Here, get changed, it's one-fifteen."

After giving her seal of semi-approval to my appearance she walked with me as far as Mr. Lumley's door. She patted my arm and wiggled her fingers in my direction as she trekked on down toward the dining-room-turned-Bingo-parlor for the afternoon's games. "Promise to tell me how it goes."

Mr. Lumley promptly answered my knock and led me into his Spartan living quarters. Furnishings consisted of a lot of chrome. A glass-topped chrome table around which sat four chrome swivel chairs covered with plush black leather was the main focus of the apartment. The place resembled a conference room more than a living room.

I stared at the world map I had seen earlier; it was the only color in the room. Pushpins poked into it in numerous areas of the world. "Are you charting the cook's culinary travels?" I joked.

A smile crossed his lips but didn't reach his eyes. "No, geography is sort of a hobby of mine."

Yeah, right, I thought.

I continued gazing at the map and tried to determine which countries he had pinpointed. I'm not much of a geography buff, but I noticed most of the pins were poked into European and mid-eastern countries. His melodic baritone voice broke my geographic concentration. "The Mihshi Malfuf today was not bad—almost authentic flavor, actually."

My ears perked up, but I attempted to keep my face a mask of unconcern as I turned to face him. "Really? It was my first taste of Saudi food. I take it you've eaten it before?"

He ignored my question, came to my side and gestured across the room. "Would you like to sit here at the table? I'm afraid I have nothing more comfortable at the moment."

I sat down and placed my yellow pad in front of me. "This will be fine. Is the rest of your furniture coming later?"

He scanned the room. "No, this is about it. I travel pretty light. Got this," he patted the glass-topped table, "at the thrift store so I'd have a place to sit my laptop other than my lap."

I nodded my head. "Cozy," I lied. It was anything but cozy. It was a cold, gray place. My thoughts were more along the line of, *This is an interior decorator's nightmare,* and, *Maggie would be able to add some color and warmth in here.*

I glanced at the bookcases. "Perhaps you should invest in a recliner and a reading lamp. You have an extensive library." The titles were mostly unfamiliar, but I saw numerous books on world culture, dictionaries in foreign languages and several spy novels.

"You may be right." His voice was deep and soft. "Maybe you would consider helping me with that, since I'm new in town." He smiled again, this time it reached his eyes, and curled my toes.

I regained my voice, fumbled for my gel pen. "Uh, yes, Mr. Lumley. Now for that interview. Where, exactly, did you live before joining our Golden Harvest?"

His eyes twinkled at my joke—and my discomfort. I averted my eyes and noticed his hands had left fingerprints on the glass-topped table. He pulled a white monogrammed handkerchief from his pocket and carefully scrubbed them away. "I'm a citizen of the world, Helen." He cocked his head. "May I call you Helen?"

I nodded, too unsure of my vocal response to open my mouth.

He continued. "Unfortunately, it's been an adventure of the mind. I'm an accountant—from Boston. Retired."

My face must have registered some skepticism, because he hastened to add, "Do you remember the Thurber character, Walter Mitty?"

I nodded, wondering where that question came from. "He was the guy who had big dreams about doing great things which came to life in his mind. They made a movie about it back in the forties."

"That's right. The Secret Life of Walter Mitty. Danny Kaye played the lead. I have a great respect for anyone who aspires to greatness, don't you?"

I shrugged. "I suppose," I said, still unsure of the direction of this topic.

He spread his arms wide. "Well, Helen Patterson, meet the real-life Walter Mitty."

I jotted a few notes on my legal pad. Lumley had a secret life, all right, but he was definitely *not* Danny Kaye. This guy would bear further checking.

In an attempt to get the conversation back on track, I asked, "An accountant, you say? Our administrator, George Hardestee, was an accountant—a wonderful CPA—for years. Did you know him, by any chance?"

He folded his arms across his chest and leaned back comfortably in his chair. "You mean *former* administrator, don't you? I hear he's been replaced by the Carmichaels."

I shot him a questioning stare. "Their name is Cunningham but, yes, that's true. How did you know?"

His head gave an ever-so-slight involuntary shift. "Right. Cunningham." He reclaimed his nonchalant attitude, and shrugged. "Word gets around."

"Yes, it does." But I wondered how he had picked up the information so quickly.

I doodled several question marks on my legal pad before continuing the interview. I looked into gray eyes, which suddenly masked any feeling, and said, "I'm sure all the ladies here would be interested to know if there is a Mrs. Lumley lurking about somewhere."

The smile he gave softened and relaxed his rigid features. "My wonderful wife, Eileen, passed away many years ago. After her death, my work became my life."

I continued to gaze into those eyes and acknowledged, without a doubt, his devotion to his wife; that look was unmistakable, I'd seen it often in Maggie's eyes as well as in George's. I finally managed to utter, "Maybe it's an accountant reaction. After George's wife died he also immersed himself in his work. He never felt the need to re-marry, either." I chuckled. "He finally begged my friend, Maggie, and me to stop trying to find him a replacement spouse."

He smiled again. He had a really nice smile when it reached his eyes. "Yes, well-meaning friends can be a problem. Was that your friend Maggie sitting at the lunch table with you?"

"Yes," I answered, "she and I have known each other forever. It's nice having my dearest friend living in such close proximity."

"Lovely woman," he said. "I must admit, now that I'm retired I miss having someone, a friend," he hastily added, "with whom to share the day-to-day adventure of living. Friendship is a very strong bond."

Lovely woman, huh? So he had noticed Maggie. I tucked that tidbit away until I could figure out a way to introduce him to my friend—maybe! Perhaps I should warn her to stay as far away from him as possible. Aloud I said, "I don't think I will divulge the bit of information about friendship in my article." I raised my eyebrows in what I hoped was a teasing manner. "Unless, of course, you want a constant parade of old, but eligible, women knocking on your door in the guise of 'just wanting to be friends'."

He held up his hands in protest. "Please, no. That was definitely off the record. I normally don't wax so nostalgic. Must be the move—or your journalistic skills."

He winked. Okay, were those eyes laughing at me or flirting?

He continued, "I have noticed some of the ladies around here are..." he hesitated.

"Like vultures circling carrion?" I intoned.

"Well, that's not exactly how I would have phrased it, but

yes." His deep, baritone laugh might have tipped the scales in his favor, if I hadn't had so many other questions about his secretive behavior. Yes, Mr. Lumley would definitely bear watching!

He glanced at his watch. "Well, Helen, I hate to rush you away, but I have an appointment to get a haircut." I glanced up as he rubbed his hand across his salt-and-pepper military buzz cut. It didn't look to me like it needed cutting.

He rose, came around the table to help me to my feet and grabbed a sport jacket as he walked me to the door. "Do you have enough information to make me appear interesting?"

I tucked my notes into my bag. "I suppose I can do something with what you gave me," I said.

"Good. Perhaps one-day next week we can go check on that recliner," he said as he closed and locked the door behind us. I walked with him as far as the front door, where he made his exit.

I turned and rushed to find Maggie. Accountant, indeed. Foreign language dictionaries, push pins in exotic places on a map, and a CEO's work area didn't shout accountant to me. Add to that his knowledge about the new administrators, and his twitch of discomfort at calling them the Carmichael's by mistake. AND he had eaten original Saudi food! I had a feeling Maggie's Mr. Lumley was involved in the mess at this place up to his mysterious gray eyeballs.

TRADITIONAL MIHSHI MALFUF

(stuffed cabbage leaves)
2 lbs. cabbage (1 med. Head)
1 cup uncooked rice
1 lb. lamb shoulder, finely chopped
1/8 tsp. cinnamon
1/4 tsp. allspice
Salt and pepper to taste
4 large cloves garlic
1 T. dry mint or 2 T. fresh mint
1/4 cup lemon juice

Core and parboil cabbage until limp and easy to roll. Place in a colander and separate leaves. Slice each leaf in half on the ribs. If ribs are large or coarse, slice part of rib off. Leaves should be roughly 4" long and 6" wide.

Mix rice, meat and spices. Place a tablespoonful on each leaf. Spread lengthwise along rib and roll as for jelly roll. Gently squeeze each roll when placing in pan. Arrange in compact rows over a layer of cabbage ribs. Sprinkle a little diced garlic between each layer. Cover rolls with water ½" higher than the top layer. Sprinkle 1 tablespoon of salt over top. Place a pottery plate over cabbage so the rolls will remain firm and intact. Cover pan and cook on medium heat 15-18 minutes.

Mash one clove of garlic with mint and a little salt. Add lemon and mix thoroughly. Pour over entire top of cabbage and simmer for 20 more minutes, or until rice is done. Serves 6-8.

Pat Pratt

EASY MIHSHI MALFUF: SAUDI ARABIA

2 lb. cabbage (one med. Head)
1 cup uncooked rice
1 lb. ground beef
1/2 cup butter, melted
1 tsp. salt
1/2 tsp. pepper
1/2 tsp. cinnamon
I med. Onion
1 can tomato soup
1 cup water

Combine rice, ground beef, butter, salt, pepper and cinnamon; mix thoroughly. Form into small rolls. Cook individual cabbage leaves in a small amount of water until wilted. Wrap around rolls and place in heavy skillet. Add tomato soup and water; bring to a boil. Cover, simmer for 45 minutes. Yield: 6 servings.

Chapter 12

Is That Your Final Answer?

Maggie was more than a little skeptical about the conclusions I had come to concerning Mr. Lumley. I had arranged myself on her settee and she ranted as she paced back and forth in front of me.

"Really, Helen, how could you believe Mr. Lumley might have anything to do with getting George replaced?"

I reached for her arm. "Maggie, slow down. I didn't say that."

She pulled her arm away, put her hands on her hips and glared at me. "You said he was mixed up with the Cunninghams. It's the same thing!"

I shrugged. "Maybe. But let's think about this for a minute. He showed up like some nomad at the same time they did—and he's got that world map with all the pins in it. Not to mention all those foreign language dictionaries."

She sat down daintily and folded her hands in her lap. "What does that prove?"

I ignored the question and checked my notes. "And don't forget he knew all about that moofle stuff we had for lunch. He said it tasted almost authentic." I pointed my pen in her direction.

"How many people do you know who have tasted authentic Saudi Arabian food?"

Maggie grabbed the legal pad. "So what you are implying is that George's termination is the result of some kind of covert international spy business."

I studied the age spots on the backs of my hands. When put that way, my conclusions seemed a bit outlandish. Without looking up I whined, "But he has all those spy novels."

"Yes, and you have a shelf of cookbooks and you can't even *pronounce* mihshi malfuf, let alone cook it!"

She was right about that. I loved browsing through cookbooks. The pictures and recipes always looked so tempting, but I'd never been much of a cook. Dinners at our house had been predictable, easily prepared, fare—preferably from a box or can. At holiday time I lit pumpkin or apple pie scented candles or, for the grandkids, the sweet smells of chocolate chip or sugar cookie candles permeated the air. My offspring swore if I ever started filling the house with the waxy aroma of baked ham or turkey and dressing, they would disown me. So maybe Maggie was correct about Mr. Lumley; he might be what he claimed, an armchair traveler—but I had serious doubts.

Maggie continued to hammer away with her debate. "And what about 110? Mrs. Warner just moved in, too. Do you think she's mixed up in your conspiracy?"

"Okay, okay, I get the point. You win." I paused and pointed at her, "although, wasn't Mata Hari an exotic dancer?"

Maggie shook her head and raised her arms in defeat. "I give up," she sighed.

"Good." I may not have won that battle, but I had at least

forestalled it. "Let's focus on our number one problem—the Cunninghams."

We decided an interview for the newsletter would at least get us some preliminary information. I told Maggie I needed some back-up for the encounter.

"What do you need me for? You are perfectly capable of conducting an interview."

I grabbed my legal pad from her—I felt insecure without it—and appealed to her balanced nature. "This is a very touchy subject. George has been a friend for forty years, and I don't trust myself to not pop their heads off—or, at the very least, say something that will blow our cover."

Maggie laughed. "Blow our cover? Sounds like you've been reading Mr. Lumley's spy novels. But I see what you mean; you do tend to get a little carried away. I'll go with you to keep you in line." She glanced at my well-proportioned mid-section and raised her eyebrows. "Horizontal prison stripes wouldn't do a thing for your hips."

Mature individual that I am, I stuck my tongue out at her.

We decided on a few key questions, then she stood up, claiming she had to go freshen up for dinner. I told her she looked fine to me, and asked whom she was trying to impress. Even though she always 'freshened up' before meals, I thought there was more to it than that. I feared she had taken more than a passing interest in Lumley, and I wondered how I could discourage her. I didn't trust him, and I didn't want my friend to be hurt.

On my way to the dining room that evening I passed Annie,

our recreation director, prowling around in front of one of the apartments. Her eyes darted furtively up and down the hallway and when she saw me she suddenly turned and hustled away without so much as a how-do-you-do. She didn't even offer an invitation to the next bingo party. Strange! There sure was a lot of odd behavior going on around this place.

I stopped by the administrator's office to set up an appointment with Jamie Cunningham for three-thirty the following day. I paused and sniffed the air for alien vibes. I had no idea what they should feel or smell like, but was glad no ET's jumped out at me.

After dinner of Moo Goo Gai Pan, which I determined to be a bit bland, Maggie and I returned to my apartment. We spent the evening composing questions for the Cunningham's that might give us some insight into the pair's objective.

Ora was just leaving as we approached the office the next afternoon. "Thank you, Mrs. Price, Mrs. Cunningham and I will hang your decoration on our door this evening," Jamie said. Ora beamed at him like a child who has just been awarded a gold star by the teacher. The look she gave Maggie and me said, "Leave him alone, I saw him first!" It is true what they say: some old people revert back to their childish ways; they want to be the center of attention, and don't want to share things—or friends. Well, she didn't have to worry; I didn't intend to 'steal' Jamie Cunningham from her. But, I thought, when I uncover whatever he and Frankie are up to, and bring them down, Ora is not going to be happy with me. Well, then, she could stand in line behind the rest of the disgruntled people in my life.

We followed Jamie into the office. He carelessly tossed the wreath on top of a file cabinet and motioned for us to sit down.

"The crafters are creating projects in honor of our international theme, and Mrs. Price brought us a nice door decoration," he explained. "Are you ladies in the crafting group?"

Maggie opened her mouth and I elbowed her in the ribs. I was not here for idle chitchat, and I wasn't going to let Mr. Jamie Cunningham try to get us on his good side. As far as I was concerned, he didn't have a good side. I answered with a curt, "No", as I maneuvered my chair so it was positioned directly across from him.

"I wasn't expecting a visit from both of you lovely ladies." He turned his mouth up in a serpentine smile.

I stared across the desk at him. I could only describe his face as cadaverous: long and skeletal, deep-set eyes, thin lips over which sallow skin stretched tight. Maggie had laughed when I pointed out my observation to her earlier in the day. She told me my perception was obviously clouded by my feelings. She said he was actually quite handsome. Yeah, I had answered, in a nether-worldly sort of way. Today he was dressed casually in slacks, short-sleeved shirt and loafers, and I swore I heard his bones rattle when he sat down and propped his feet on the desk.

It wasn't until we were seated that I noticed Frankie on the far side of the room peering through her large-rimmed glasses over a pile of file folders. Her dark hair was pulled into a tight French knot—that's probably why her eyes bugged out behind those glasses. The eyes themselves were unnerving, their color a light hazel, almost yellow. Cat eyes, I thought. And she looked at

Maggie and me as though we were mice on which she was preparing to pounce. The part of her I could see was dressed in a tailored white blouse and tweed jacket. I assumed she also wore matching tweed slacks; she always dressed in severely tailored, manly looking pantsuits. She reminded me of a matron from an orphanage in those old novels—not merely a strict taskmaster, but really mean because she could be.

There was no doubt in my mind who was in charge in this relationship—whatever the 'relationship' consisted of. Obviously she was here today for Jamie in the same capacity as Maggie was for me. She glanced at a spot somewhere between us and gave us a cursory nod before returning to her work. I think she also ran her tongue across her whiskers.

I produced my pen and doodled a snake, a skull and crossbones and a large-toothed cat on my legal pad. "So, Mr. Cunningham, what brought you to Golden Harvest?"

He rested his arms on his chest. "We were approached by the state to do some financial updates on various enterprises, and Golden Harvest was on that list. It's a formality—something the state mandates periodically."

Frankie rustled some files and Jamie clammed up.

"So you and Mrs. Cunningham are like auditors?" I continued.

He drummed his fingers on the table. "My, uh, wife is the certified auditor, but I also have degrees in accounting and management."

I pressed on, irritation showing in my voice. "I see. How long have you been doing this sort of thing?"

Frankie jerked her head up, and Maggie cleared her throat.

70

"What Helen means, I believe," she said, "is this your first retirement home audit?"

Frankie glared somewhere over my right shoulder and Jamie relaxed. "As a matter of fact, it is."

"How long do you intend…" Maggie stepped on my foot and I stopped and rephrased my question. "How long does a process like this generally take?"

Frankie stood up and patted the stacks of papers on the desk. "As you can see, there are many files to go through. Such things are a matter of utmost privacy and cannot be discussed. The information will be turned over to the state after we make our determination."

I stood up, turned and faced her. "George Hardestee is as honest a man as I've ever met. You will find nothing the least inappropriate in any of his dealings!" I, swiveled back, leaned into Jamie's face and rested my fisted knuckles on his cluttered desk. He and Maggie jumped up, too. We resembled a quartet of tag team wrestlers waiting to be tagged in.

Jamie held his hands up in front of him. "Now ladies, you can be sure the intent of this audit is not to discredit Mr. Hardestee. It is a formality, as I said. I understand and sympathize with your affection for the man, but the state requires these periodic audits." He motioned to our empty chairs. "Could we all please sit down and finish the interview?"

Except for Frankie, the wrestlers returned to our respective corners. She jabbed her red pen in my direction. "You do understand that you must not allude to anything in that article except that this is exactly that, a periodic audit. Nothing more!" She curled into her chair, retracted her claws and grabbed another folder from the stack in front of her.

That sounded like a subtly veiled threat to me, but Maggie kicked my shin and I nodded.

I bit my lower lip, took a deep breath and continued. "Are you from this area, Mr. Cunningham?"

He leaned back in his chair, glad the volatile situation seemed to have been averted. "No, and please call me Jamie—and my wife, Frankie. I find first names create a sense of camaraderie—of family, if you will."

Family, indeed! Skeleton Jamie "Bones" and his cat-wife would never be a part of my family. I cleared my head and throat and continued through gritted teeth, "So, Jamie, where are you folks from?"

He smiled. "Frankie and I travel a lot. This business keeps us on the move. Last year we were in Connecticut. We also spent some time in South America auditing an international business. You might say we are citizens of the world."

Startled by that comment, I dropped my pen on the floor and turned abruptly to Maggie. She raised her eyebrows. That's exactly what Mr. Lumley had said!

I used my foot to wrestle my pen within reach, bent down to pick it up and asked, "What do you do in your free time? Checking figures all day has got to get boring, and hanging around senior citizens can't be all that stimulating."

His eerie laugh sent cold shivers down my spine. "Nonsense, Mrs. Patterson, doing something you love is never boring. But you might say I'm a collector of sorts."

"Oh? What do you collect?" Maggie asked.

"A few stamps and coins from our travels. Nothing big or

exciting. A small hobby at best."

Frankie coughed and Jamie took a sudden interest in his watch. "Dear me," he said, "I just remembered a call I must make, and it's after four. Will you ladies excuse me, please?"

We rose to leave and as we reached the door I turned and said, "By the way, Mr. Carmichael?"

"Yes?" he answered before he realized the slip up.

I caught the blink and twitch in his right eye. "Have you ever eaten authentic mihshi malfuf before?"

"Uh, no, no, I don't think so. Why?" he stammered.

I smiled sweetly. "Just wondered. Thank you for your time, Jamie." I peered over his shoulder and gave Cat Woman my sweetest smile. "You too, Frankie."

We hurriedly left their lair. Neither of us said a word as we headed back to my apartment to discuss the progress we had made. I mentally noted the absence of antennae and heavy make-up to hide telltale green skin tones on the suspected aliens. Perhaps my expectations had been colored by too many Hollywood productions. Like Lennie, I had also felt some currents in the air around the office, but attributed them to hostilities of the human kind.

It was an hour before we had to report to the dining room for dinner, so Maggie and I hurried to her apartment to organize our thoughts on the interview with our new administrators. Maggie was still skeptical of the conclusions I had come to. Even the Cunningham/Carmichael slip-up of the new administrator didn't convince her; but I was more sure than ever.

After our evening meal, a forgettable fare, except for the peach upside-down cake, reminiscent of a cakey peach cobbler, we returned to my apartment to continue our discussion.

Maggie prepared two cups of lemon zest herbal tea while I read through my notes. I was sure Jamie and Frankie were up to something, but I wasn't sure where Lumley fit into the equation. I'd have to do some more sleuthing eventually, with or without Maggie.

As she set our drinks and the sugar bowl on the table in front of me, I scooped two spoonsful of sugar into my cup, stirred it into the steamy liquid and said, "Maybe I should take your Mr. Lumley up on his invitation to go chair shopping."

Maggie slammed her teacup down so hard I feared she had cracked the saucer. After a quick scan to assure the china was intact, she muttered, "The saucer isn't broken; *and* I wish you would stop referring to the man as *my* Mr. Lumley, he doesn't even know I exist."

The fact that she phrased her response in that particular way was not lost on me. Perhaps I could do some matchmaking—If Elsworth Lumley didn't turn out to be in cahoots with the Cunninghams, of course.

She was still checking the saucer for chips. I touched her arm, "Don't worry about that saucer, Maggie, it's fine."

She placed it on the end table without looking up.

I continued. "Why don't we think of some pretense to go into town and invite your—invite Mr. Lumley to accompany us? We could quiz him some more under the pretext of looking for some furniture for his place."

She continued to stare at the teacup as she nervously wrung

her hands. "Oh, I don't know, Helen." She looked up at me. "It doesn't seem right, somehow."

Her mouth said no, but her eyes said something else, so I kept pushing. "Come on, it will be fun. You want to look for some of those Comfort Zones like Elsie's, and McClain's furniture store is just down the street from the department store."

I grabbed her hands, for fear she would rub the skin off with her incessant wringing of them. "Why are you so nervous? It's not like we're asking him out on a date or anything." She pulled her hands free and I continued, "Although we could take him to lunch, or maybe pie and coffee, at the Downtown Café. A piece of Mable's pie might loosen his lips."

Maggie looked at her hands, now folded in her lap, and I barely heard her response. "Pie would be nice."

"Right. With two of us talking, maybe we can distract him so he will slip up like Jamie did, and say something incriminating."

She glared at me. "I think you are completely wrong about Mr. Lumley, so I'll go along with your little game just to prove it!"

"Fair enough," I nodded; but I was concerned that if he were mixed up in this mess, all would not be well between Maggie and me.

PEACH UPSIDE-DOWN CAKE

Batter:
1 cup flour
1/2 cup sugar
2 tsp. baking powder
1/4 stick butter
1/2 cup milk

Combine all ingredients, mixing well. Put batter into 8X8 baking dish.

Fruit mixture:
Peaches halves, canned or frozen
1 cup sugar
Nutmeg to taste
1 cup water

Combine all ingredients. Pour over batter. Bake at 375% for 50 minutes. Cake will rise to top and fruit will be on bottom. Yield: 6 servings.

Chapter 13

You Could Have Knocked Me Over
With a Feather

After Maggie left I sat down to work on the newsletter. My interviews with Mr. Lumley and the Cunningham's were so short that, even with the poem Elsie Barstow had submitted, I didn't have enough material to finish out page four. Like *Reader's Digest*, I had resorted to funny anecdotes at the end of each piece, but there are only so many fillers you can use in one newsletter. I decided to drop in on LeeAnne Warner the next day to extend a welcome to Golden Harvest. Her interview might warrant page one attention if I could get her to talk to me about her 'career'. I had a few scarves of my own, but had never attempted to dance with them. And I cringed at the thought of the number of peacocks and ostriches that would have to be de-feathered to create a fan large enough to conceal my ample frame.

I was still puzzling how I was going to breech the subject when I knocked at Ms. Warner's door at ten-thirty the next morning. I don't know what I expected, but was more than a little disappointed when she answered the door wearing a shocking pink sweat suit. My mother would have had a few choice words about that 'fashion faux pas'. "No young lady with red hair should ever wear pink or orange, and no girls with blonde hair should wear yellow," according to my fashion-police Mater.

Throughout my formative years I thought that coordinating hair and clothing choices must be the first of the ten fashion commandments. I never saw them, but I was sure my mother and all her cronies had copies of the fashion codebook tucked away somewhere. They all referred to 'those fashion disasters' when they verbally dissected women outside their circle.

I was one of mother's fashion failures. Try as she might, she couldn't keep me clean and pressed, and finally gave up on me when I was about five. She began asking me to please not come storming into the house while she was entertaining visitors. I think they all pretended I belonged to the gardener or the chimney sweep.

But, regardless of my mother's rules, Ms. Warner looked lovely in her casual wear, the red hair in question pulled into a loose ponytail that couldn't quite contain her thick, naturally curly locks. Wavy tendrils framed her face and gave her a bouncy, youthful appearance. She was taller than Maggie, about five-three or four, her eyes were green and very large, and appeared even larger because of the thick false eyelashes and heavy green mascara that highlighted them. The sweat suit did little to hide her curvaceous figure; I was instantly jealous. The jacket zipped to her neck as though she was just leaving for a morning jog or workout. Perhaps she had been working on her makeup, her face was clear of blemishes and smooth of wrinkles and gave no indication of her age. Must be good makeup, or she wasn't as old as I thought, I decided. Discreet lady that I am, I was not about to ask. I peeked past her—no fans or feathers or scarves in sight.

I thrust out my hand and she took it a bit hesitantly. "Mrs. Warner. Hi, I'm Helen Patterson."

"Hello," she answered. Her voice, the words spoken in muted tones, was deep and reminded me of ocean waves rolling onto the beach. That voice contradicted my preconceived notion of a loud and raucous woman strutting around on stage. I was somewhat astounded and continued to hold her hand, unsure how to end the contact.

In my left hand I carried my yellow pad and some back issues of the newsletter. I pushed the latter in her direction, as much to break the sensation of awe as to explain. "I write a paper called The Harvester here at Golden Harvest. It features current and coming events, poems and stories by the residents, and maybe a joke or two." I paused for a breath while she leafed through some of the issues.

I continued, "I like to include introductions about our new tenants to help us get better acquainted, and this has been a busy week."

She looked up at me, green eyes sparkling. "Really?" It hadn't been my imagination. Her voice really did sound like soft breaking waves, even though I had to strain to hear what she was saying. I couldn't believe this shy, quiet woman was the same woman Sophia had claimed she was.

She continued to scan the newsletters while I stood in the hall waiting for an invitation into her apartment.

"Yes, there's you and 122, a Mr. Elsworth Lumley."

Her head jerked up at the name and she looked up and down the hall.

"Do you know Mr. Lumley?" I asked.

"No, no," she stammered, "but it is an unusual name, isn't it?"

"Yes, it is. I've already talked with him and, if I could have a few minutes of your time, your interview would round out my newsletter for this week."

"Well, I don't suppose it would do any harm," she whispered. "Come in. You will have to excuse the mess, I'm not completely unpacked."

She was obviously joking; the place was immaculate, no papers or mail strewn on the table, not even a cup or dish in the sink. It looked better than mine and I'd been here for nearly a year. There were no packing boxes in sight, pictures already hung on the walls, all straightly aligned. In a small corner grouping, surrounded by fresh-cut flowers, sat a hand-painted oriental urn. Her husband probably reposed inside that vase, I decided. The thought of keeping a husband in a vase held some grotesque appeal; at least you always knew where he was and whom he was with. A shadowbox to my right caught my eye. In it were two ticket stubs, a playbill, one peacock feather and a pair of theatre glasses. Aha! Evidence of her scandalous past, perhaps?

I smiled at her, mentally assessing how she would look in feathers. "Your apartment is lovely, Mrs. Warner. I'm afraid I have no skill or desire to decorate. You have done a great job."

A faint, "Thank you," emanated from her lips.

I continued, "If it weren't for my granddaughter, Ellyn, my walls would all be bare, I'm afraid. Do you have grandchildren, Mrs. Warner?"

Another shy smile crossed her lips. "Please call me LeeAnne."

"Thank you, LeeAnne," I answered. "And why don't you call me Helen?"

"Alright, Helen. To answer your question, no, my husband and I never had children. Charlie traveled a lot, and I," she paused, bit her lower lip and stared off into the distance, "I also worked at that time. By the time things settled down for us we were too old and set in our ways to start a family." She sighed. "At least that's what we told ourselves."

She shook her head. "But you aren't interested in all that melodrama, I'm sure. Come, sit by the window, the light is much better over here." She led me to her sitting room and I seated myself in one of a pair of comfortable-looking armchairs positioned on either side of the window. The one I chose was royal blue, the other a dusty rose. To one side and finishing out the grouping was a small loveseat upholstered in a royal blue and rose flower print fabric. Throw pillows, that picked up the colors in the two chairs, were scattered about. I sat back; the chairs were as comfortable as they were attractive.

LeeAnne, now the relaxed hostess, asked, "Could I get you something to drink? Juice perhaps?"

"Yes, thank you, juice will be fine."

She went to the kitchenette, pulled two stemware glasses from the cupboard, filled them with some orange concoction she had in a juicer on the counter, and handed me one. Her hands were delicate, her nails neatly manicured.

"Fresh vegetable juice," she said. "It's very good for you."

I held the thick cloudy liquid up to the light. The stuff had two strikes against it—fresh-squeezed vegetables and the phrase, "it's good for you"; two things guaranteed to spell disaster. Nevertheless, I took a sip. It had a rather sweet flavor, although somewhat chewy texture. I pretended it was a malted milkshake on the verge of turning. "Not bad," I lied.

She smiled. "It has carrots and..."

I held up my free hand. "Please don't tell me. I'm sure I'm better off not knowing. Kind of like the ingredients in all those international dishes cook has been preparing this week."

She laughed. "I know what you mean." Her voice was either gaining strength or my hearing was getting better. "My husband and I, as I said, traveled most of our married life so I have been exposed to the cuisine of many cultures, some better than others."

Yes, the voice was definitely gaining confidence. I set my juice on a coaster and reached for my notepad. "What business was your husband in, LeeAnne?"

She held out her right hand, showing a ring that might have blinded me given the proper lighting. "He was a diamond appraiser and gem cutter in the international market."

I pulled her hand close so I could get a better look at the multi-faceted beauty. "Is this real?"

Her laughter became a low lyrical sound that caused me to look up into those green eyes. Suddenly I could imagine her on the stage, and her voice, now that it had grown stronger, was mesmerizing.

"Yes, it's real. Charlie indulged me with all sorts of baubles like this. I guess it was his way of making up for being on the road so much."

"I hope you have them insured and under lock and key. Or better yet, in a vault somewhere," I said.

She laughed. "No vault, but I have a lockbox in my closet. I like to keep them close. I know they are just things, but having them with me keeps Charlie close." She blushed. "Does that sound terribly vain and silly?"

I cleared my throat and considered how nice it would be to have shared that kind of love. "No, not at all."

I searched for the right way to pose my next question. "And you said you also worked for a time?"

"Yes, that's right."

Where to go from here? "Was your position with your husband's company?"

She lowered her eyes and shook her head.

I decided to try another approach. "I also worked. I managed an insurance agency, and after the loss of my husband it was the only thing that held me together." No sense going into the details of that loss. Maybe she would spill some things about her past out of sympathy for what should—oops, could—be my dead husband.

She remained silent, so I went right to the forward approach. "LeeAnne, I hope you won't take offense at my brazenness, but I heard that you were once on the stage. Is that true?"

She rolled her eyes, sipped her juice, and stared down into the dregs of her glass. "Goodness, that seems like lifetimes ago. It *was* lifetimes ago. I gave it all up for Charlie. Yes," she sighed, "but what a lifetime."

"Were you on Broadway?" I blurted out.

That melodious, husky voice answered. "Not exactly; I was a dancer. But it's funny you should bring it up. There was a skit I did in my act that had a character by the name of Elsworth Lumley. When you mentioned that name earlier, a lot of memories came rushing back. I can't believe there is actually someone by that name—and that he lives just down the hall from me!"

Now, that's an interesting twist, I thought. I hastily wrote the information on my legal pad. She reached over and touched my hand. "I hate to sound like a snob or anything, but could you perhaps say something like 'she chose love over what might have become a promising career'?" She flashed that shy smile again, and wrinkled her nose. "Or something of that sort? I'd not know what to do or say if a lot of people started pressing me about my 'past life'. Charlie was my life—my one true love. Anything else in my life meant very little."

No weeping or desperation in her voice, just a simple, straightforward request. I patted her hand that still rested on mine. "Of course, LeeAnne." And I realized I meant it. I liked this lady. I'd have to introduce her to Maggie. She was, unlike my original mental image, not brassy, but classy.

I'd sure like to find out the juicy details of her career, though. Not for the newspaper—just to satisfy my curiosity. I was, I must admit, in awe of LeeAnne Warner. Other than Janine Hopgood, I'd never before known anyone who had been on the stage. Besides, I was curious how one went about twirling those feathered fans.

Chapter 14

Make new Friends-
What about the Old?

The article about LeeAnne finished out my newsletter. It had been tastefully done, if I do say so myself, and even Maggie complimented me on its content. By merely alluding to her career, I seemed to have piqued everyone's interest in Ms. Warner. The article caused quite a stir around the place. Some, like Ora and her cronies, complained to me that the woman was 'putting on airs'.

"You know how those people are," remarked Ora. She had cornered me on my way to the library, and proceeded to rattle off all the inside information she had picked up from her 'reliable sources'.

"What people are you referring to, Ora?"

"Why, all those Hollywood types," she said with an exaggerated sweep of her arm. "You wouldn't believe the way those people carry on. They attend wild parties and stay out until all hours. And the way they outfit themselves is absolutely disgraceful! They traipse around half dressed in those bikini things. Why, in my day, a lady did not show her skin to the whole world.

We were wholesome and discreet in our apparel and our manners."

I placed my hand on her shoulder in a gesture that belied concern. Actually I only wanted to get past her and into the solitude of the library.

"Ora," I spoke in my most sincere voice, "you read too many trashy movie magazines; and you believe everything you read in that newspaper you subscribe to. What is it, Insider Lies?"

"Insider *Eyes*, Helen. Eyes, NOT lies," she fumed. "And those investigators know what really goes on in the world." She looked up at me defiantly and shook an arthritic finger in my face. "We must always be prepared! It's a scary place out there, Helen."

I stepped around her. "Some days it's no Shangri La in here, either," I mumbled. "Now if you will excuse me, I have a date with a book."

She started to step back in my way, but seeing the glare I gave her, moved to one side. As I opened the door she said, "A book date is the only kind of date you are apt to get. You read those *trashy* mysteries, but know nothing about the *real* world or the people in it!" With that, she flounced unsteadily down the hall.

If Ora represented the real world, I'd take my chances with nursery rhyme mysteries any day.

On the flip side of reactions was Janine the Snow Queen. On the day the article came out she was on the phone to me as soon as she retrieved her copy.

"Helen, you must introduce me to Mrs. Warner," she oozed in the voice she generally reserved for her theatrical encounters.

"Why me, Janine? Introduce yourself."

"Oh, I couldn't do that," she said.

"Why not? I've never known you to be shy before."

She stammered, "But Ms. Warner was a star. I wouldn't know what to say."

I paced the floor, phone to my ear. "For crying out loud, Janine. It's not like she's Betty Davis or Marilyn Monroe. March up to her and say, 'Hi, I'm Janine the Snow Queen and I'm here to save your Christmas.'"

Janine began whining in her pouty voice. "You're being mean, Helen. You were always jealous of my performance!" With that she slammed the phone down in my ear—thank goodness. I couldn't take much more of the Snow Queen's dramatic histrionics.

After a few days, Janine had finally gotten up the nerve to introduce herself to LeeAnne, and now hounded the poor woman on an almost daily basis to help her initiate a drama club. So far LeeAnne had resisted, but she admitted to Maggie and me she was running out of excuses.

I had introduced Maggie and LeeAnne and they had hit it off immediately, as I knew they would. The three of us began a leisurely camaraderie that developed into a friendship. We had a lot in common, not the least of which was the ineffable Janine.

"The woman is relentless," LeeAnne said one day as we were visiting in her apartment. "She refuses to take NO for an answer. I find myself sneaking around to keep from running into her."

I picked up a piece of Brie and a cracker as I walked past the counter. "Maybe you could get a restraining order against her as a stalker."

Maggie poured juice and handed us each a glass. "Helen, be nice. Janine is stage struck—always has been. She still lives in the glow of her high school performance."

I raised my glass. "It was junior high; how long can she bask in that glow? The batteries in that light ought to be dead by now." I was not nearly as willing as Maggie to excuse the Snow Queen's behavior. I feared we would eventually be subjected to the reenactment of some better-left-dead-and-forgotten classic. "I can see it now. Janine as some consumptive starlet boring us to death while in the throes of coughing herself into oblivion."

"Stop that, Helen," Maggie chided, as she put the back of her hand to her mouth to stifle a laugh.

LeeAnne pointed in my direction. "I have an idea. Maybe I should suggest to Janine that we do a comedy revue and you could headline, Helen." She winked conspiratorially at Maggie. "I could put in a good word for you."

"Don't you dare. I've avoided that woman for over fifty years and I'd like to keep it that way."

"Face it, Helen," said Maggie, "you avoid everyone except me—and now LeeAnne." She smiled and motioned to our new friend.

"And for good reason. Most people are annoying—and that goes double for Janine."

LeeAnne placed her tray of cheese and crackers on the table and we all sat down to enjoy our snacks and some relaxed conversation. Maggie had brought grapes and fruit juice and I contributed fig bars. I swear those things were multiplying in my cupboard; I couldn't seem to get to the end of them.

LeeAnne and Maggie were both tastefully dressed in Capri pants, Maggie's in one of her many shades of blue with an ocean-print cotton blouse, LeeAnne's in hot pink with a white blouse bearing a matching hot pink flower bedecked with sparkly sequins.

"You two look very springy today," I commented. "Did you coordinate those outfits?"

Maggie laughed. "It *is* spring, Helen. You should try some capris. They're quite comfortable. I could shorten the legs of those pants you have on and you'd be set to go."

I was wearing my hibiscus outfit. "You leave my pants alone, they are fine the way they are. This fabric is all-purpose and doesn't wrinkle. Besides, my figure isn't suited to those cut-off things." I liked my thrift store purchase; comfortable wash and wear colorful enough to not show random food stains works well for me. Maggie, on the other hand, was growing weary of the outfit. Oh well, she didn't have to look at it if she didn't like it.

I glared at her. "I'd like to discuss something other than my fashion sense, if it's all the same to you."

She smiled. "Fine. What did you have in mind?"

I sipped my juice. "I talked to George again, and he said he's bored to death at his sister's. She watches soap operas and court TV all day. She keeps the volume up loud enough for the neighbors to listen in because she's hard of hearing. He said he's taken to wearing earplugs to muffle the noise. He sounded really frustrated and depressed."

"That's terrible," agreed Maggie. "We've got to do something about getting his position back!"

"I know. I told him we were working on a plan to get him reinstated, but he was adamant that we stay out of it."

"Poor man," sighed Maggie.

LeeAnne had sat quietly through this conversation. "Who is George?" she finally asked.

We explained and she agreed something should be done. "I

remember talking with him when I began looking for a place. He seemed like a very caring person."

We visited idly for a while until Maggie consulted her watch, stood and gave me, and then LeeAnne, a hug. "Ladies, I hate to leave such good company, but Elsworth promised to teach me to play backgammon. We're meeting in the library at three."

I stood too, and began picking up the snacks. "Who are you trying to fool, Maggie? You taught me to play backgammon when we were kids!"

"Yes," she smiled sweetly, "but I haven't played in years."

"Um hmm," I answered.

LeeAnne, on the other hand, encouraged the woman. "Sounds like someone's caught the eye of our Mr. Lumley." She clapped her hands. "Good for you, Maggie. He must really like you. I've seen him beating a hasty retreat from all those women who have started flocking to the exercise room in their stretched-to-the-max tights."

"I certainly wouldn't stoop to anything like that," said Maggie as she bagged the remainder of her juice and carried the empty glasses to the sink.

"Yes, Maggie. You remain an enigma. The only woman here who didn't fall all over herself to make Mr. Lumley's acquaintance has managed to arouse his curiosity."

I had introduced Maggie to Lumley when we 'accidentally' bumped into him in the dining room after the piece about him came out in the Harvester. Since that day he and Maggie managed to get together on a semi-regular basis. I saw much less of her now and, to tell the truth, I was a bit jealous of the time he stole from what had, up to a few weeks ago, been Maggie's and my time.

"Right. Even you went knocking on his door, Helen," teased Maggie.

"Nonsense," I said as we finished clearing away the remnants of our snacks. "I was merely gathering news for the Harvester. My introduction to your Mr. Lumley was strictly business." As an afterthought I added, "Hey, maybe LeeAnne could come along when we take Lumley chair shopping."

LeeAnne raised her hands in protest. "Not on your life. They say three is a crowd; if that's the case, four will be an intimidating mob. I don't want to scare him away from Maggie." She touched my arm. "Could I speak to you for a minute, Helen?"

Maggie waved. "I'll see you girls at dinner," and she walked down the hall, a distinctively new bounce in her step.

I turned and asked, "What's the problem, LeeAnne? You seem concerned about something."

She wrung her hands as if unsure what to say. "Well, Helen, I know I've only known you and Maggie a short time, and I hate to interfere, but…"

She paused for so long I began to get antsy. "But *What*? What's the problem?"

She took hold of my arm again. This woman was getting pretty familiar for a new acquaintance. "I thought maybe you should let Maggie and Mr. Lumley go alone to pick out a chair."

"Why? It was my idea in the first place. I thought Maggie might like to come along. I wanted to pump him for information. I'm sure he knows more about what's going on around here than he's letting on."

She nodded. "Oh, I see. You like him too."

I pulled away. "That's ridiculous! I was only trying to help Maggie. I knew she wanted to meet Lumley; I was playing matchmaker, and want to be sure he's on the up and up."

LeeAnne held out her hands open like a book as if to show me items one through three of the senior dating manual. "Then why not let them go alone and get better acquainted? I believe Maggie is smart enough to know if Mr. Lumley is sincere."

I was not yet willing to give up. "But it was my idea," I whined, as I again reached for the door.

She tossed me an indulgent smile and patted my shoulder. "I know, but at least think about it, okay?"

"Yeah, sure," I said. But, as I trudged back to my apartment, my thought was that my best friend had formed a new alliance. Lumley claimed most of Maggie's free time. She had drawn him and LeeAnne into her circle and I felt I had been left on the outside looking in.

Chapter 15

Marvin's Missing Meerschaum— Ernestine's Evasive Elgin

I took the long way around to my apartment and decided to stop by the library. More research, I told myself; It certainly wasn't to spy on Maggie and Lumley! I wanted to check out the latest nursery rhyme mystery by my favorite author. I love her protagonist, whose name just happens to be Helen, like mine. She works in a children's library although she hates kids, and spends her spare time scanning newspapers to find crimes to solve. She recites nursery rhymes while she whips up on the bad guys using her master karate chops and kicks. Actually, I think my alter-ego Helen takes out her frustrations about those kids who terrorize librarians and desecrate library books. All those people who use and abuse—the ingrates! I could identify with her rage.

I considered learning some karate moves myself, perhaps to use on the new administrators—or on Lumley, if he hurt my friend! None of those fancy high kicks though; raising my leg above my waist was not an option.

I saw Maggie entering the library as I came down the hall. She had added a lightweight sweater to her outfit, thrown casually over her shoulders. I stopped and peered into the glass-enclosed room. Lumley stood as she approached and pulled out a chair for her. The backgammon board was already laid out on the table and he pulled up a chair to her left, so he faced the windows and the entrance—typical spy positioning, I thought. Today he wore not his signature gray, but a powder blue sport shirt suspiciously close to the blues Maggie favored. I quickly moved on lest he think I was watching him.

As I reached the door I was distracted by an insistent male voice calling my name. I turned to see Marvin Oglevie limping in my direction, his ebony cane with silver hand grip tapping with each step. He was dressed in a tweed smoking jacket complete with leathered elbows. He was ensconced in the aromatic scent of cherry-blend tobacco that always followed his faltering gait. He reminded me of a character from a 1940's drawing room one-act play.

"Helen," he wheezed, as he approached. "I'm glad I caught you. My favorite Meerschaum is missing."

I scowled at him. "Well, I certainly don't have it. As fond as I am of the aroma of fine tobacco, I never took up the pipe-smoking habit."

"Of course not," he laughed nervously, unsure whether or not I was joking. "I wasn't accusing, I merely wanted to ask if you might put a note in your next newsletter in case someone should find it."

"Oh, sure, I could do that." I removed my notepad from my pocket and scribbled down the information. "When did you first miss your pipe?"

He sat heavily on one of the overstuffed chairs in the alcove across the hall from the library entrance, so I made myself comfortable in the other.

"Yesterday morning," he said. "I always place it in the pipe stand beside my easy chair. I know we're not allowed to actually smoke in our apartments, but the feel of it between my lips relaxes me while I read my morning paper. When I reached for it yesterday, it was gone."

Okay, so Marvin needed a pacifier while he read, not too weird. Nonetheless, I grilled him, as any good reporter would do. "Could you have left it somewhere?"

He shook his head. "No, I'm very careful about my pipes. Besides, I already checked in the smoker's gazebo, and it wasn't there. I asked some of the other smokers, and no one had seen it." He wrung his hands and ran his arthritic fingers over his balding pate. "I'm sure I put it back in the pipe stand." He sounded desperate; anyone listening would have been convinced someone had stolen his life savings.

I continued. "Have you had any visitors?" Marvin was a widower, but I had it on good authority that he entertained more than occasional company, although I would never pass judgment. I certainly did not have first-hand knowledge of the fact, nor would I spread rumors. However, word had it he received late night visits from various females in the place.

"Absolutely not!" He paused, then added, "Not in the last four or five days anyway. Mrs. Halverston..."

"Please." I held up my hands, "I'm only interested in events at the time of the disappearance." The thought of Marvin and Mrs. Halverston—or any of the other ladies in question—in the throes of whatever it was they did in his apartment, made me shiver. I returned to my senses and asked, "Was anything other than your pipe missing?"

He thought for a moment, and then shook his head. "No, but I did notice something strange." He stared through the library windows so long I followed his gaze. He was watching Maggie and Lumley, who seemed to be enjoying a very amusing game of backgammon. I had never realized it was a comical game, so what were they laughing about? I forced myself back to the business at hand.

"Well, what was it?"

He looked at me like I was some alien who had just appeared in the chair beside him. "What was *What?*"

I was beginning to think Marvin was off his noodle—or maybe off his meds. I'm afraid the irritation might have shown, ever so slightly, in my voice. "What was strange the day you misplaced your pipe?"

"Oh, that. Well, on the table by my pipe stand there was a small dish."

"A dish? What sort of dish? Something you brought from the dining room?" I was getting more and more irritated. Maggie was in the library having a grand old time with Lumley while I sat here listening to Oglevie discuss place settings.

"No, nothing like that. This was a small leaf-shaped bowl, or maybe a little ashtray, about this big." He put his fingers together forming a small circle. "I had never seen it before. It was white with gold trim, and on the bottom was stamped Occupied Japan."

"So you're saying a thief took your pipe and left an ashtray? Do you see the irony in that? Perhaps someone is playing a practical joke."

He seemed startled by that possibility and couldn't think of anyone who would do such a thing--or why. When I asked to see the leaf dish, he said fine, but he didn't see what good it would do.

Even though the possibility existed that Marvin was simply hallucinating, I agreed to add a lost-and-found column to my next newsletter. I pulled myself out of the chair and promised him as much, made my excuses and headed back across the hall to the library.

As I reached the door I noticed Lumley's hand resting on Maggie's, and she was making no attempt to undo the situation. I wasn't sure what game he was playing, but it sure didn't look like backgammon to me. I turned and stomped back toward my apartment. I needed to finish my newsletter anyway.

Maybe I would just go find a new friend myself. LeeAnne was out, she had already sided with Maggie. I thought of Kate McGinnis, she was always trying to get me to attend some fool thing or another. She and her husband, Stanley, had moved to Golden Harvest about a year ago, just before my offspring had shuttled me here. They were one of the few couples that inhabited the place; most of us had come here to escape being old, alone and broken down in our old and broken-down homes.

According to Maggie, Stanley had taken early retirement and arranged for his and Kate's position here. He had worked long and hard all his life and now longed for the leisurely comfort of doing nothing. He was happy to be free from the responsibilities of home-ownership and all that it entailed. His wife, he reasoned, who was a joiner of clubs and civic organizations, would find the close proximity of women of similar age and status a good match for her outgoing nature.

As it turned out, also according to Maggie, the move was a better fit for Stanley than for his wife. On the "outside", as she incessantly reminded those who would listen, she had been hostess to many events—chair-person of the Garden Club, a member of the Historical and Genealogical societies, art club, book club, to name only a few. If her city, or any city within driving distance, held any type of meeting, she tried it out. But at Golden Harvest, everyone had their own agendas, leaving poor Kate without a group to chair.

Kate was a short, round woman with chubby red circles for cheeks, puffy hands and ankles, and feet crammed into shoes two sizes too small. I wondered once how she had managed to get her feet into the shoes and decided she must have put them on before she started to swell up. Everything about her suggested an over-inflated beach ball. She had brought me a write-up to put in the newsletter about her latest crusade, something about antique jewelry. When I questioned the need for such a group she said, "Most of the ladies here have some fine old jewelry. We could research the pieces and date them—perhaps discover some interesting background on them."

Still skeptical about the objective of such research, I asked, "But why? Who really cares?"

"Helen Patterson, I'm surprised at you." She shoved her right hand toward my face. "See this?"

How could I not see it, she barely missed poking my eye out with a large, gaudy ring.

"Uh huh," I replied.

"I'll have you know," she huffed, "this once belonged to the queen!"

"Oh?" I mumbled. She didn't say what queen. It might have been the Queen of Hearts who had lost it in her tarts, for all I knew—or cared.

Kate had continued waving the thing in front of me. "Think of it like genealogy—discovering who your ancestors were by the jewelry they handed down to you."

"Well," I told her, "my ancestors gave me a Timex for graduation, my husband bought my engagement ring at the local discount jeweler. After he left, I sold it to get the toilet fixed. The way I see it, my ancestral jewels are pretty much flushed."

She had chuckled in spite of herself, and had handed me the article. "I would appreciate it if you could put this in the paper, perhaps it will generate some interest. I am somewhat of an expert. Perhaps I could at least research individual pieces for people."

I had put it in last week's paper, but hadn't heard of anyone rushing off to have Kate check his or her ancestral gems. After all, how many people here could have inherited jewels from the Queen of Hearts?

Maybe, I thought as I continued to my apartment, Kate and I could start a book club. I decided it never would work, the woman was way too opinionated and always had to have the last, if not the first, word. I really hate people like that.

I toyed with the possibility of kindling a relationship with myopic Wally Cox—a frightening, desperate prospect. But I finally came to the conclusion, as much as I hated to admit it, that Maggie was right; the majority of the world was too darned annoying for me to want to have anything to do with them.

Aftermath of the lost-and-found article created a backlash of conversation and speculation. Ernestine Pelletier informed me her watch was missing. "It was an Elgin," she said. "My late husband, rest his soul, gave it to me over twenty years ago. I thought I might have misplaced it, but your article caused me to believe someone might have taken it."

"What made you change your mind?" I asked. We were all aware of Ernestine's mild dementia. She tended to forget the most mundane things at times—like losing her glasses when they were hanging by the chain around her neck, or getting dressed up and leaving on her bedroom slippers. Nothing serious, just another of those mild irritations we all have to look forward to in our 'Golden Years'.

"Well," she said, "I always lay my watch on my nightstand— always in the same place, beside my glasses, so I can find them. The other day when I reached for it, there was a little cut glass bird in its place."

"A glass bird?" I asked. "Was it yours?"

"No," she said. "I had never seen it before."

"Do you still have the bird?"

She shrugged. "No, I seem to have misplaced it too," she apologized.

Several others had similar experiences to report. Adele Quartermane's address book was replaced with a packet of foreign stamps, Frank Gordon's flashlight with a tulip nightlight and Sarah Matlock's symphony guide with the weekly TV magazine.

This pilfering business was getting curiouser and curiouser, as Alice once said. But we weren't in Wonderland and I didn't think the White Rabbit was responsible for this rash of disappearances.

Chapter 16

To Market, To Market

My curiosity won out over my irritation with Maggie and LeeAnne, and I called them later in the week to come to my apartment for a conference. My door was soon graced with Maggie's familiar, annoying shave-and-a-haircut knock, and when I opened it, she and LeeAnne breezed in. Maggie headed for the kitchenette and said, "Good company and cryptic phone calls demand food." She opened the cupboard and pulled out my fig bars. "Helen, these have to go!" She unceremoniously dumped them into the trash.

LeeAnne laughed and added, "They are a bit like Gobstoppers—they're never-ending!"

"Looks to me like Maggie put an end to them," I huffed. "I happen to like my fig bars."

Maggie took a plate from the shelf and reached into the canvas shopping bag she always carried; that was my friend, always doing her part for the environment. I wasn't sure how environmentally sound it would be to introduce those never-ending fig bars into it, though. She pulled out a fresh, crackly package. "See, macaroons. You love macaroons."

101

"And I brought white chocolate macadamias," added LeeAnne. She held up her package like a trophy.

"Fine," I grumbled. Actually, macaroons and macadamias are two of my favorites, but I had to maintain my cranky attitude, they expected it; and I wasn't ready yet to completely forgive her and LeeAnne for shutting me out. Besides, they were having way too much fun at the expense of me and my fig bars.

I stomped to the fridge to show my displeasure about the disposal of my cookies. "I suppose you want me to furnish something to drink." I checked the refrigerator, pulled out three mini cans of ginger ale, which I placed on the counter. "It's either these or tea or instant coffee." I opened the second cupboard door. "Or I have a half bottle of wine."

Maggie said, "How about the coffee?"

LeeAnne, ever gracious, said, "Whatever is easiest."

I grabbed the electric teapot, filled it with tap water and plugged it in, while Maggie extracted three cups from hooks screwed under the cabinet. She opened the jar of coffee and shook it. "Helen, dear, do you have a sharp knife? These coffee crystals seem to have—uh—crystallized."

I looked into the jar and handed her a spoon. "Here. Scrape it with this. It breaks up easily."

Maggie tentatively scratched at the congealed crystals before setting the jar on the counter. "On second thought, let's have tea, shall we?" She reached for the small wooden box that held my tea bags. "Jasmine sounds good." She plopped a bag into each cup and added water from the kettle, which had begun a high-pitched whistle.

LeeAnne, in the meantime, had arranged cookies on the plate, and we took our cups and sat around my small table.

LeeAnne daintily picked up the macaroon I had my eye on—the one with the most toasted coconut—and nibbled the edges. "So, Helen, what's the big powwow for? You sounded mysterious on the phone."

I grabbed the second toastiest macaroon and set it in front of me. "Well, there's something really strange going on around here." I munched my cookie and sipped my tea. LeeAnne and Maggie leaned forward; both clasped their hands together in front of them, and patiently watched as I slowly chewed and swallowed my treat. When I reached for a white chocolate macadamia cookie, Maggie grabbed the plate. "Oh, no! Not until you tell us what is going on that is more strange than usual."

She knew I'd give up state secrets for another cookie. I recounted what I'd discovered about the missing objects, and they listened without interruption. Maggie sat motionless, LeeAnne rested her elbows on the table and cupped her chin in her hands. "Sounds like a practical joke to me," she said.

"Yes," agreed Maggie. "But to what purpose?"

"I thought at first it was a joke, too," I said, "but the more I think about it, the more convinced I am it's part of something bigger. I think it's tied to whatever Frankie and Jamie are up to."

Maggie looked at LeeAnne and rolled her eyes. "Oh, oh. Here comes another conspiracy theory." She turned to me. "So what is it you think they are up to? And what would playing practical jokes have to do with it—whatever IT is?"

I had to admit I hadn't figured that out yet.

I read them the list I had made of the stolen items.

"Allegedly stolen," Maggie intervened.

"Right," I said, "*allegedly.*"

Marvin's Meerschaum had been replaced with an ashtray, Adele's address book for stamps, Sarah's symphony guide for a TV magazine, and all the others. We noticed each had something in common, the items began with the victim's first initials, and each had some relationship to the missing item—Marvin's pipe for an ashtray, the address book for stamps, and so on. It all fit until we got to Ernestine's Elgin. We couldn't figure out the connection between the watch and the bird. The initials matched, but what did the bird have to do with anything?

Finally, LeeAnne jumped up and clapped her hands—that annoying habit of hers—probably held over from all those fan-dancing standing ovations. "I have it! Time flies."

Maggie and I stared at her. "Time flies? That's it?" I said.

She shrugged. "Have you got anything better? Maybe the joker is evolving—becoming more ingenious with the game." She folded her arms. "But why those particular people? What do they have in common?"

I spoke up. "They're all a little senile."

"Helen," my guests said in unison, both stifling a chuckle. "That's not nice," Maggie finished.

"But true," I pointed out. "I know Marvin never locks his door. And Ernestine is so forgetful she probably can't find her door key half the time. If we check, we'll probably discover the others don't keep their doors locked either."

"Okay, but what does that have to do with the missing items?" asked Maggie.

I got up and paced back and forth. "Well, the perpetrator has to gain entrance to the apartments somehow."

Maggie grabbed my arm. "Sit down," she demanded. "That annoying habit of yours is making me nervous!"

I plopped back down and scowled at her. "I don't have any annoying habits."

Maggie patted my hand. "If you say so."

LeeAnne asked, "If it is the Cunninghams, as you suspect, why wouldn't they just use their master key? They have access to any of our apartments any time they want."

I drummed my fingers on the table while I considered that. Maybe Maggie could keep the rest of my body in place, but my fingers could still prance. Finally, I said, "They probably don't want suspicion to come back to them. If they only go into rooms that anyone can get into, they are in the clear."

Maggie, ever logical, said, "But there is no reason for them to do such a thing. I think it's a practical joke, a silly game one of the residents is playing. It's a little devious, to be sure, but no real harm has been done."

I leaned back and folded my arms on my chest. "Not so far, anyway."

Maggie went to the kitchen, returned with the reheated kettle and warmed our tea. We let the subject drop, content to enjoy each other's company with small talk. Finally, Maggie rose and said she needed to go change before dinner. She looked fine to me. As I picked up the cookies, I asked if she had any clothes that weren't in shades of blue.

She looked from her neatly pressed outfit to my weathered attire. "I happen to like blue. And you are a good one to question anyone about fashion. Where is your hibiscus outfit, by the way, in the laundry?"

I brushed across the front of my blouse in an effort to spruce it up. "Yes," I mumbled. I looked into her twinkling blue eyes and one corner of my mouth curled up in an involuntary smile. "I happen to like my hibiscus outfit."

She laughed and patted my arm. "I know. But we really need to update your wardrobe. Don't you agree, LeeAnne?"

LeeAnne shook her head and held up her hands in protest. "Oh no, leave me out of this. I'm all for comfort over style. If Helen is comfortable with large flower gardens billowing behind her as she walks, let her be."

I checked her expression. "Was that comment an affirmative to me or to Maggie?" I asked.

She smiled. "What do you think?"

"I think," I said as I popped one more macaroon into my mouth, "that you two are ganging up on me."

"As a matter of fact, Helen," Maggie said, "El thought tomorrow would be a good day to go shopping for that chair. I might even look at some slacks or skirts in green or hot pink. We could shop for some spring clothes for you, too. He asked what time we wanted to head out."

I glanced at LeeAnne who raised an eyebrow in my direction. "I don't need any new clothes," I grumbled. "Besides, I have some things to catch up on tomorrow," I lied. "You two go without me. If I make a list, could you pick up a few things for me while you are out?"

LeeAnne noticeably relaxed, Maggie smiled and said, "If you're sure. Don't forget to put coffee on that list," she added, as she dumped my coffee jar in the trash with my cookies.

If I weren't careful, she would clean me completely out of

food. I nodded. "Absolutely. And more fig bars."

They both groaned.

As I walked them to the door I kept my eyes on Maggie. I was concerned about her; I could tell she was very infatuated with Elsworth Lumley. I swore to myself that if he hurt her, I was going to have to hurt him.

But right now I had other things to worry about, like what Frankie and Jamie were really up to.

Chapter 17

Home Again, Home Again

Maggie and Lumley went on their romantic shopping trip the next day. She argued, rather feebly, I thought, that I should accompany them. I declined and instead, sat in my apartment and sulked.

LeeAnne called to check on me and suggested we get together for a friendly game of gin rummy. I told her I didn't feel the least bit friendly, and if she brought any gin it had better be in a glass with tonic. She tried to cajole me into good humor, but I said I needed to catch up on my reading. I had checked out that nursery rhyme mystery, "Mary Little is on the Lam", but, try as I might, I couldn't concentrate on it. I put it down, picked up my legal pad and charted everything I could remember about the strange goings-on, starting with George's suspension.

I tried to figure out what Frankie and Jamie had in mind, and to connect them with the stolen goods. None of the residents who had so far lost items had anything in common except possible dementia. And, as far as I knew, none of them had anything worthy of this elaborate scheme. At least nothing of great value had come up missing. All I was sure of was that the

Cunningham's were mixed up in this petty larceny.

I read through the statements again.

Number one. Marvin liked the ladies, although he sometimes inadvertently invited more than one for an evening nightcap. When that happened, he would set up the Scrabble board and spell his way out of the predicament.

Number two. Ernestine, as we all knew, constantly misplaced things and was, in general, a tad ditzy.

Number three. Adele had a book full of addresses. She sent cards to anyone and for any occasion, obvious or obscure. Of course, one might get a Christmas card in July or a Valentine on May Day, but she was consistent in her mailings. I once received a Happy Groundhog Day card from her in June. The fact that it actually arrived on my birthday, the eighth, was, I'm sure, a coincidence.

She even sent notes to the president, although I'm not sure she even knew the name of the current Commander-in-Chief. She addressed the cards to 'Mr. and Mrs. President', so I guess it didn't matter. However, she is probably on a government watch list somewhere; anyone who sends Christmas Cards in July, or Gopher Greetings any time of the year must be instantly suspected of something.

None of the other alleged victims on my list provided any further clues. So, although it was said as a joke, the only thing I could see they all had in common was their forgetfulness, and that's no reason or explanation for a crime. If it were, we would all be incarcerated.

I tossed the pad on the table and picked up my library book. At Maggie's familiar knock I jumped and the book dropped to the floor with a thud. Dazed, I looked down. Great, I must have fallen asleep mid-sentence, and now I had also lost my place. I groaned as I bent to pick up my book, pulled myself up and lumbered to the door.

Maggie practically glided into the room. She had come by to deliver the supplies on my list and inform me about her "perfectly wonderful day with El". She was so bubbly I asked if she was intoxicated. She patted my shoulder then turned to empty the grocery bags and put the items in my cupboard. "Helen, don't be such a grump. You could have come along."

"I didn't want to get in the way," I mumbled.

She puttered so long with my goods I asked if she was alphabetizing them or sorting by size.

"I'm arranging things neatly. How do you ever find anything in here?" she asked as she pulled things out and placed them on the counter.

As she scrutinized each item and stacked it back in the cupboard, I said, "I open the door, look until I see what I want, then reach in and get it. Pretty easy, really. It's not like any world-changing decisions are made based on how fast I can find my coffee. In fact, sometimes I just close my eyes and grab—I like surprises."

She turned to me and smiled. "You do not. You hate surprises. But it's a good thing no national security depends on your canned goods arrangement, because your cabinet screams 'Anarchy reigns!'" She gestured to the newly arranged shelves like a beauty queen showing off a prize showcase on some game show. "Now, isn't that better?"

I had to admit with all the labels facing forward, things were easy to spot, but I was used to my chaotic arrangement. "Won't last long," I grumbled. But I had to smile when she raised her eyebrow at me; I couldn't stay angry with Maggie, she was my best friend.

I sat down at the table. "So tell me about your shopping trip," I said.

She told me she and 'El' had picked out a swivel recliner and 'El' had added a small glider rocker with matching ottoman. Both were in steel gray—naturally—although the glider had flecks of blue.

"He said the blue matches my eyes," she beamed.

Yup, I would have to kill 'El' if he broke my friend's heart.

After a long sigh, Maggie trotted starry-blue-eyed to the table. She poured two glasses of ginger ale and sat one in front of me while my mind wandered off considering ways to do away with Lumley.

"So what did you do today?" she asked, barging into my reverie.

I blinked, returned to the conversation, and retrieved my legal pad. We perused the outline and she agreed that the information didn't add up too much.

"Maybe you're mistaken about the Cunninghams," she said. "I'm concerned about their appearance here, too, but they haven't done anything wrong."

"Except steal George's job," I reminded her.

"Well, yes, there's that. But they gave a legitimate reason for that. Even George said what they did was within the guidelines of state codes. It isn't a crime to audit a business. And stealing small items from the apartments seems like a silly practical joke, not some big conspiracy. What would be the point of them doing something so petty?"

She was making a good argument. But I had a bad feeling about those two; I just had to prove I was right. I couldn't convict them on a hunch. Whatever they were up to, I knew it was no practical joke.

Maggie shook her head. She had known me too long to believe she could change my mind, so she changed the subject.

"I bought a pink outfit today, and a pale yellow print sundress. El said I looked like a Maui sunrise."

I bristled. A letter-opener to the throat should kill him, I thought. The next thing I knew, Maggie hollered my name and jumped up. I jerked back to the present and watched my glass roll across the table. Ice cubes and ginger ale soaked into my lap. The afore-mentioned letter-opener had materialized into my hand and I dropped it on the table as I came out of my chair.

She returned from the kitchenette with a couple of towels. "What in the world were you trying to do?" she asked as she sopped at the mess.

"What?" I said as I grabbed one of the towels to wipe cold, sticky liquid off my pants. "Oh, I was thinking about something, and I guess I bumped my glass."

"It looked to me as though you were trying to stab something. Remind me not to make you mad—at least not when you are within reach of any sharp object."

She rinsed the towels, handed me one, and continued wiping. "What were you thinking about?"

I faltered. I couldn't very well tell her I was daydreaming about putting a letter-opener to Lumley's throat. "Oh, this whole mysterious business, I guess. It's got me puzzled. I don't know what to do next."

I mopped up the floor and handed her the towel. I picked at my soggy outfit. "Actually, what I need to do next is get into some dry clothes, if you will excuse me."

Maggie rinsed the towels one more time and draped them over the sink. "Go ahead. You definitely need to change. I'll catch you at dinner."

As she reached the door she said, "You know, Helen, this isn't one of your mystery novels. I think you're trying to create intrigue where there is none. Worrying about the Cunningham's motives seems to be making you a bit," she paused, "well, a bit crazy. Maybe you should drop the whole thing."

My crazed, drippy self stopped mid-step and argued in a not-quite-insane voice, "Crazy? You're the one who decided we should figure out what was going on, remember? I wouldn't have started working on this Cunningham problem if you hadn't brought it up!"

She nodded. "I know, and I'm sorry." She patted my arm condescendingly. "Maybe you should relax and work on something else for a while."

With that she walked out the door. I slammed it behind her and stomped to the bathroom, soaked and angry, mumbling, "A bit CRAZY? I should RELAX?"

She was right to be concerned for my sanity, though. Between these break-ins, the usurpers to George's throne, Maggie's involvement with 'El', and her alliance with LeeAnne, I was becoming more unstable by the minute!

Chapter 18

A Tisket, A Tasket,
I Found It in a Basket

I remained reticent through dinner. While Maggie and LeeAnne nibbled their food and discussed wardrobe, furniture and Lumley, I munched on my salad and soup, devoured my roast and managed to steal Maggie's cherry cobbler without her even noticing.

Finally, LeeAnne turned to me. "You're awfully quiet tonight, Helen. I apologize if I've monopolized the conversation."

I waved my spoon at her while I chewed and swallowed a mouthful of Maggie's dessert. "Heard it all this afternoon," I said between bites. "Pink outfit, yellow dress, Maui sunrise, blah, blah, blah."

The hurt in Maggie's eyes said it all. I'd gone too far—again. I lowered my gaze to the half-eaten cobbler in front of me. "Sorry, Mags. You know how fashion-unconscious I am. Look at me!" I had donned my freshly-laundered hibiscus outfit after my ginger ale shower. "Your idea of a bargain is ten percent off the rack at Macy's, mine is everything you can stuff in a bag for a buck at the Nifty Thrifty."

They both nodded emphatically. I frowned in their direction

114

and continued. "I'm sure you are lovely in your yellow sundress, but just try to imagine me in it. I wouldn't look like a Maui sunrise, I'd look like the sun rising over a Maui Mountain!"

I smiled and they burst out laughing. Maggie touched my hand across the table. "Helen," she said, "that's not true. But you do paint a vivid picture."

"Yes," agreed LeeAnne, "you are the Van Gogh of verbal put-downs—at least about yourself. Haven't you heard? Big is beautiful."

"Right," said Maggie.

That was easy for them to say; those were not comforting words coming from two lightweights. The fact is, it would take both of them on the other end of the teeter for us to totter! Nevertheless, I shoved the half-eaten cobbler in Maggie's direction. "Would you like some dessert? It's delicious."

She looked around for her own bowl.

"It's also yours. I borrowed it while you two were having your fashion discussion."

We all had a good laugh. I was forgiven once again.

The next day I wandered around the garden attempting to come up with something interesting to add to this week's newsletter. I had hoped to find Sophia out there puttering, she was always good for some juicy tidbits. The weather was mild, with an earthy, spring aroma. Today was light sweater weather, and Maggie would soon be able to make use of that Maui sundress. It was a perfect day for Sophia to be out digging in the dirt. I needed her to dish up some good dirt for me; it was a really slow news week. I sat on the stone bench in hopes she would float by and, at the same time, hoping Wally-in-the-box wouldn't pop up. Sophia couldn't be far, her basket of gardening tools was sitting right here beside me, a small shovel-thing, a claw object with sharp pointy tines, her gardening gloves, all with her initials, 'SG', neatly written on them.

Then I noticed something tucked in the fingers of one of the gloves – a small gargoyle or some sort of grizzled face grinned up at me. I bent down for a better look, checked right, left and behind me, reached in the basket and grabbed it. Marvin's Meerschaum! The hand-carved bowl bore the likeness of the head of some misshapen little man, perhaps a leprechaun that, I swear, winked at me as I cradled the pipe in my hands. I glanced around again and stuffed the tiny gnome-headed pipe in my pocket, stood up and made my way back into the building.

I should return it to Marvin, but first I had to consult Maggie. I lumbered to her apartment, banged on her door and rushed in when she opened it. She ventured a peek out into the hall before closing the door behind me.

"What in the world is wrong with you? The way you pushed your way in, I thought someone must be chasing you down the hall."

I reached into my pocket, pulled out the pipe and handed it to her.

She turned it around in her hands, inspected it from all angles. "Is this Marvin's pipe? Did you take it? Helen, what is going on?"

I grabbed it back. "Of course I didn't steal Marvin's pipe. I found it!"

She took my arm, led me to a chair and sat me down and, after seating herself beside me, calmly asked me to explain. I told her about Sophia's gardening basket.

"Do you think Sophia took it?" she asked.

116

I shook my head. "I don't know what to think. Sophia is a bit strange, but she doesn't seem like a thief."

Maggie picked up the phone. I grabbed her hand. "You aren't going to call and ask her, I hope."

"No, silly," she said as she plinked out the number. "I'm calling LeeAnne. We need another perspective on this. If two heads are better than one, imagine what three heads can accomplish."

"Yeah, but what happens lately is that you two get your heads together, and I feel like a third wheel."

"Nonsense!" She patted my hand as she put the receiver to her ear. "LeeAnne. Hi, this is Maggie. Why don't you bring some of those macadamia cookies and pop over to my apartment. Helen has a development to discuss about our mystery. Great. See you in about five minutes."

She put the phone down and took my hands. "Helen Patterson, you have got to get over the idea you are being replaced. Third wheel, indeed! Why, what would a tricycle be without three wheels?"

I looked at my hands. She had them tightly clasped in hers, as if I might bolt and run. "Tricycle?" I mumbled.

"Yes, tricycle. And as long as we're using that analogy, you would be the front wheel—the big one with the pedals and the go-power. LeeAnne and I bring up the rear and come along for the ride."

That sounded pretty good. I raised my head and smiled. "Front wheel, huh?"

"Definitely." She gave my hands a final squeeze and let go. "You know you will always be my best friend; we have experienced far too much of life together for that to change. We

117

know way too much about one another for me to break in someone to take your place."

She stood up, leaned over and gave me a big hug. I've got to say, there's nothing like the embrace of a good friend to make you feel special. I thanked her and gave her a big bear hug in return.

Knuckles lightly tapping on wood announced the arrival of the third wheel of our trike, and LeeAnne breezed in, cookies in hand, neatly arranged on a blue and white platter—Blue Onion pattern—not some cheap knock-off, the real thing. She casually plunked it down on the coffee table.

She brushed her hands together, stood up and tucked her red hair behind her ears. "Okay, girls, what's up? More mysteries to solve?"

Maggie moved to the kitchenette and pulled three wine glasses from the cupboard. "Helen will fill you in while I pour us something to drink."

I explained to LeeAnne about finding Marvin's Meerschaum in Sophia's gardening basket. Maggie handed each of us a wine glass; the golden champagne colored clear liquid danced with bubbles rising from the bottom of the glass as though it had been laced with seltzer tablets. I took a sip, the fine mist of exploding bubbles tickled my nose and the flavor was sweet and fruity.

"What is this, Maggie? Are you trying to get us tipsy?" I took another sip; it was really good, and I felt a heady rush.

"Do you like it? It's sparkling grape juice." She raised her glass. "To the Tricycle Girls. Long may we ride."

I peered into my glass and sniffed. The bubbles made me sneeze. "No alcohol? I swore I was getting light-headed."

She shook her head. "Not a drop. Disappointed?"

"A little," I said.

LeeAnne passed the cookies around. "Who are these Tricycle Girls we're toasting?"

"Inside joke," said Maggie, after which she explained the tricycle simile—me as the power driving the thing, her and LeeAnne along for the ride. The explanation served to expose more of my insecurities, and I squirmed in my chair. LeeAnne smiled and nodded. I finally managed to speak. "So, LeeAnne. What's your take on this pipe I found?"

She thought for a moment. "Sophia doesn't seem like the type of person who would be responsible for this silliness. Besides, I know she is smarter than to leave evidence laying around if she took something."

I took another cookie. "Exactly what I told Maggie. Someone must be setting her up to take the fall for this caper."

Maggie nearly choked on her fake champagne. "Take the *fall* for this *caper*? Honestly, Helen, you sound more and more like a cheap novel. You need to expand your reading enjoyment."

I scowled and she continued. "But we still don't have a clue who that someone might be."

I removed the pipe from my pocket and winked back at the little gnome. "I have a whole list of who's, I just haven't figured out why."

LeeAnne got up and poured us all some more bubbly. "Maybe we should all keep our eyes open to see if and when and where the other missing items show up."

She was right. Within a week, all the stolen items had turned up in strange, but obvious, places. The address book was found in the library, the watch on the finial of a lamp in the lounge. It was like a huge scavenger hunt or crazy "I Spy" game. Everyone was having a high old time, chatting among themselves, hoping they would be the next person 'chosen' for the 'Lost-Personal-Property' game.

Some game! I told my granddaughter, Ellyn, to bring me my golf clubs. I no longer played the game, but anybody who snuck into my room was going to get a close-up of my nine-iron if I caught them attempting to pilfer something from me.

Chapter 19

Called to the Office

With my clubs under my bed I felt much safer. I tried to convince Maggie and LeeAnne to each borrow one for protection, but they declined. Maggie said she would be too frightened to even think about swinging a golf club at any intruder, and LeeAnne made the observation that all the items had been taken while the residents were out of their rooms. That was a pretty good argument, but I still kept my nine-iron handy.

For several weeks all was quiet. We returned to our mundane existence—the crafters crafted, Bingo players hit their jackpots of fresh fruit, cookies or quarters. Maggie spent more and more time with Lumley and, at last count, LeeAnne owed me forty thousand dollars in Gin Rummy winnings. Could I help it if the woman kept begging to go double or nothing?

I skulked around after the Cunninghams for a while but got bored. I even googled their name on the Internet and got a site dedicated to actors from the old "Happy Days" show. My investigation stalled.

One day Annie, our director of coercion, called me to her office. As I mentioned earlier, Annie James was the new director

121

of activities at Golden Harvest. In the short time since she had swooped into the place, a constant barrage of tours, projects, games and day trips had assaulted the residents, at least those who allowed it. The whole elaborate ruse was like summer day camp for seniors. But the way I saw it we were moving steadily from the autumn into the December of our years with seemingly no end to Annie and her activities. The mere reading of her events calendar was enough to wear me out. All the pursuits were geared, she had explained in a community meeting, to keep us spry and socially engaged; it was unhealthy for people to sit in their respective apartments day after day. I was one of the few who had managed to not get caught up in her activity net.

As I reached her door I got the same nervous queasiness in my stomach as when I used to get called to Principal Larchmont's office in junior high school. Nothing good ever came of that, and I was sure nothing in my best interest would come of this meeting, either.

Annie's office was directly across from George's—technically, the Cunningham's now—at least until I figured this mess out. Unlike Lennie, I experienced no electrical surges as I passed by. The door was closed. George had always observed an open door policy—he wanted to be accessible to the residents. If Frankie and Jamie were in, they were being very secretive. Annie's door stood ajar, but what she referred to as her 'office' was a desk in the craft area. She had claimed one corner of the room when she took the position of recreation director.

She met me at the door of the cramped rec-room dressed in her standard uniform of long gathered skirt over which she had draped a loose-fitting blouse, all covered by a long sweater vest.

She always dressed in black or some other dark, muted color. Annie was in her forties, short and plump; the elongated outfits were meant, no doubt, to give her a taller, thinner appearance. I recognized the attempt—I had tried the same trick for years to appear slimmer, but finally decided it wasn't working and wasn't worth the effort. I ran my eyes over her outfit; it wasn't working for her, either. Today she wore dark purple and resembled a giant eggplant; but I wasn't going to tell her, she would figure it out one day. I pointed to the over-sized brooch she had pinned on one shoulder. "Nice pin," I said. "Is that an amethyst?"

She clapped her hand over the pin. "This old thing? No, it's costume." She gave a self-conscious laugh. "I love jewelry, but who can afford the good stuff on my salary?"

She pointed to a straight chair, asked me to sit down and settled herself behind a small desk pushed into a corner to my left. I took note of the rest of the packed room. Two long tables formed an el on the back wall and to the right. The tables contained easels with paintings in various stages of completion. The place smelled of oil paint and turpentine. Today was senior art day. I'm no artist or professional art critic, but, although some of our residents may be as old as Grandma Moses, I could tell at a glance none of them had her talent. Canvasses depicted vases of flowers, a landscape or two, a British flag—at least I think it was British—some Tory in the group, I guess. One rendering looked like it might have been created by that famous elephant—you know the one--he sells his trunk-paintings to raise money for the local zoo. I pointed to it and asked if the painters were doing a charity event for the zoological society. Annie shook her head. I guess she didn't get the joke.

"No," she said. "I called you here because I thought since

spring is in the air we should have a 'Spring Fling'. I would like for you to write about it in your little newsletter so everyone can start preparing."

Little newsletter, indeed! My little newsletter amused me more than her 'little' Bingo parties or the 'little' painting projects she arranged for the residents. I thought of Maggie's insistence that Annie wasn't a bad sort, really. She wanted everyone to join in some fun things; but it irritated me that she tried to suck me into her scheduled events—I couldn't get it through her head that I wasn't a joiner.

I pulled out my legal pad and jotted down the particulars. It would be like a senior prom she said; everyone could come dressed in his or her formal finery. Annie said she even knew a DJ who would come and play music from the Big Band era. She clapped her hands together. "Won't it be wonderful?" she gushed.

"Oh, goody," I sighed, "a senior prom with real seniors. Cute."

She beamed, oblivious to my facetious response, merely pleased that I was in agreement with her. She clasped her hands to her chest. "I know! All the ladies just love to get dressed up in all their antique jewelry."

She fiddled with the brooch on her shirt. "I talked to the cosmetology teacher at the high school about her class coming over to do manicures and style hair. She said it would be good practice for their final exams later in the month."

"Nice," I said. I closed my eyes and pictured the results of their 'practice'. If the hairdos and gaudy fingernails I had observed around that campus were any indication of their work I, for one, didn't want any part of it.

Since I could see she was determined about this thing, I told her I would be sure to get it into the next newsletter. "What date do you have in mind for this shindig?" I asked.

"Not shindig, Spring Fling," she corrected me.

Yup. Exactly like Principal Larchmont. "Okay, whatever. When is the *Spring Fling* going to be held?"

She moved papers around so she could see her desktop calendar. "I thought May fifteenth would be nice. What do you think?"

I shrugged. I hadn't the slightest idea about, or interest in, the whole thing. But I said the weather then should be warm enough for the ladies to wear summer frocks—I threw that word in so she would think I actually knew what I was talking about, or that I cared about her blasted party. Some ladies, God forbid, might even be persuaded to don strapless or sleeveless gowns. Mentally, I pictured ladies with their drooping bosoms, their flabby arms flapping like giant, leathery wings, as they gyrated around the room. I bit my tongue and kept that disturbing picture to myself.

Annie's grating voice broke into my thoughts. "My friend, Donna Southerland, owns the Nifty Thrifty. I'll bet she would loan The Village—her term for our residence of Golden Harvest—some evening gowns for those who don't have anything dressy to wear."

My ears perked up at that; suddenly I gained a new respect for Annie; she rubbed shoulders with the owner of my favorite haunt! Maybe she could hook me up with some even better deals than I got last time. I added the date, as well as the Nifty Thrifty contact, to my information. "Is there a theme for this shin... Spring Fling?" I asked.

She stood up, walked to the file cabinet and picked up a stack of photos, leafed through them until she came to a small picture of several hot air balloons against a clear blue sky. She held it out to me. "I thought, in keeping with our featured world-wide topics and cuisine, we could title it 'Around the World in Eighty Days'. I picked up some little baskets; now, where did I put them?" She sat back down, dug around under her desk and pulled out a plastic bag. Like a magician pulling the proverbial rabbit from the hat, she produced a tiny woven basket. "I thought we could attach these to helium balloons and let them float over the festivities. All the projects we have done in our craft classes can be used as well."

So now the full extent of the world topics to which we had been subjected lately came to light. She had been working toward this Spring Fling thing all along.

I decided to throw a touch of reality at her; I asked if she had any friends who ran a senior citizen dating service.

She said, "No, why do you ask?"

I leaned forward and planted my hands on her desk. "Well, you plan to have all the ladies dressed to kill, and big band dance music, right?"

"Right," she agreed. "What's the problem?"

I stood up and threw my arms in the air. "The problem is, in case you haven't noticed, the man pool around here wouldn't qualify as a puddle. These ladies—at least some of them—will try pairing up with the most mobile of the bunch. If you aren't careful it could get real nasty real quick."

A worried look crossed her face. "Do you really think so?"

"Ha!" I said. "I don't think so, I know so. Do you remember how Ora and Ivy fought over that Bingo card last week? I was at the other end of the hall and I could hear them screaming." I sat back down in my chair and pointed my pen at her. "That's only a mini version of what will transpire when real, live men are thrown into the mix."

She nodded. "I see your point."

She thought for a moment. "Well, you will just have to make sure to phrase it properly when you write about it."

Right, I thought; and if anything goes wrong it will be because my article wasn't worded properly. Aloud I said, "You mean something like, 'Around the World in Eighty Days Spring Fling Formal Get-together—no date required, Featuring Food and Big Band Musical Stylings From Around the World'?"

Annie frowned and managed to wrinkle her whole face in the process. If she weren't careful, she would soon be in need of my skin-iron. "Well, something like that, but maybe don't say 'Around the World' so much. It sounds a bit redundant, don't you think?"

I grabbed my notes and turned to leave. How dare she criticize my writing style, even if she was right about the redundancy? "Of course I know better than to be repetitious. That was merely the beginning of the idea," I said as I headed for the door.

Annie cleared her throat. "Helen."

I turned. "What? Was there something else you wanted to correct?"

"No." She stood and reached her hand across the desk. "I wanted to thank you. Your newsletter is a welcome asset to The Village. The residents look forward to reading it each week."

"Uh, thanks," I managed to stammer. I reached out and shook her hand. If the blasted woman kept it up, was I going to have to be nice to her? Perhaps I could be a bit less caustic in my remarks about her attempts to convert me to the glue and scissors crowd.

127

But I would NEVER allow her to deal me in for Bingo.

I left her flitting around the room humming off-key and tossing those little baskets in the air.

Chapter 20

Spring Fling-
And Lots of Bling

The Spring Fling article caused a lot of excitement around the place—at least among the ladies. They rescued their finery from bags and storage boxes—and I got a headache from the odor of mothballs that permeated the air.

Maggie knocked on my door too early on the Tuesday before the big dance. "Come on, Helen," she said when I opened my door. "We've got to find you a prom dress! Donna Southerland from Nifty Thrifty has brought some gowns to loan to anyone who doesn't own one."

"Can't I wear my hibiscus outfit? I bought it at Nifty Thrifty."

She latched onto my arm and dragged me down the hallway. "Absolutely not! The Spring Fling is a formal affair. Your hibiscus outfit is…"

I glared at her and she continued. "…well, is too informal."

I skidded to a stop, halting Maggie in her tracks. "I know it's informal. That's why I like it."

She pulled on my arm again. "Be a good sport and check out the dresses. LeeAnne and I want you at the dance with us."

129

She patted the arm she was attempting to pull out of its socket. "And what about Mr. Cox? I'm sure he would be disappointed if you didn't show up."

I pulled my arm away and stomped ahead of her. "Stop playing matchmaker for me. Fix LeeAnne up with someone and leave me alone!"

We located Donna and her dresses in the lounge. Ladies circled the two rolling racks like a herd of old, greying she-wolves surrounding a scared rabbit. They clawed and snatched at the garments with the same frenzy they showed when grappling for bingo cards.

In a panic, I turned and grabbed Maggie's shoulders. "Can we please get out of here before we get trampled or torn apart?"

Maggie laughed. "No way! We came to find you a dress. Donna has them sorted by size. Not many ladies... "

"Are as big and fat as I am?" I finished her sentence for her.

"Noooo. I was going to say as tall and full-bodied as you." She let go of my arm and gave me a hug.

We rifled through the tall, full-bodied dresses, steering clear of the grey-haired she-wolves.

The only gown that looked like it would fit me was one that hung loose from the shoulders, like a toga, but in nylon, with tiny pleats. The upside was that it had sleeves, thus covering my arms. The downside? It was, ironically, burnt orange.

"Why is it the only dress that fits me is a vague replica of that orange sherbet bridesmaid dress you made me wear for your wedding?"

"You won't forgive me for that, will you?"

"Not any time soon."

"Well, you don't have to buy this one. Donna said she will loan gowns to the ladies for the party, as long as they are returned in good condition.

I draped the orange sherbet over my arm. "I may as well buy it now. We both know my track record for neatness is less than perfect."

The cosmetology class showed up on Thursday to begin hairdos and manicures. The ladies swarmed in, as excited as kids lining up for the funhouse at the carnival, to have their hair curled and blued, and get their fingers painted. Everyone was giddy about the upcoming event—or maybe they were all high on mothballs, nail polish and permanent wave solution. I managed to wash and fluff my own hair without anyone's help.

On the Friday night of the Spring Fling thing, everyone strolled into the dining room-turned-auditorium dressed to the hilt, some of them with make-up plastered on as thick as drywall mud. Besides their evening gowns and fancy dresses, the ladies brought out all their 'good jewelry' to wear with their fancy attire.

Elsie Barstow had forgone her normal housedress and Comfort Zone slippers for black flats and a low cut gown, also in black. A red cummerbund coiled around her waist and ended up in the back tied into a large taffeta bow.

I pointed and whispered to Maggie, "How will she possibly sit down to rub her bunions with that bow draped low over her derriere?"

Maggie elbowed me in the ribs. "Be nice, Helen. She might hear you."

A diamond necklace hung around Elsie's neck and ended in

the V of what, at some earlier stage of her life, might have passed as cleavage. Now all that remained was the division, with none of the visual rewards for any voyeur who cared to look. The whole outlandish get-up was topped off, literally, with a diamond tiara.

Elsie straightened it with arthritic fingers. "I wore this at my coming-out party. It was such a wonderful gala." She sighed and her eyes glazed over from the memory—or maybe it was her cataracts that caused the glazing.

Some of the "Old Jewels" seemed to stoop more than usual from the weight of the adornments they had pinned, clasped and/or draped on their bodies. They paraded into the reception area on prom night, looking as though they had donned the entire contents of their jewelry vaults for the occasion.

"Everyone looks so lovely," cooed LeeAnne.

Maggie nodded in agreement.

I blinked at the gaudiness and waved my arms in the general direction of the overdone women. "Yeah, lots of dangly, sparkly stuff. All that is lacking are strings of lights and they could pass for Christmas trees."

Maggie and LeeAnne smiled and shook their heads. They were both beautiful in their evening gowns. Maggie dressed tastefully in a soft gown in shimmering pale blue chiffon, with a scoop neck and cap sleeves. Elsworth had bought her a wrist corsage of pale pink and blue carnations. He wore a custom-fit tuxedo and shirt with pleated front. They made a handsome pair, as my mother would say.

LeeAnne also looked elegant in a formal in emerald green with a sequined over-blouse. Her understated pearl necklace and earrings set the outfit off nicely. She had loaned Maggie a sapphire and diamond necklace and earrings, but I had resisted her offer to deck me out. I stood out enough in my orange sherbet gown.

Annie and her craft group had done a nice job with the decorations; I kept bumping my head on little hot-air balloon baskets that floated overhead. They all had candies or treats in them, but I was one of the few tall enough to notice. I offered mints to Maggie and LeeAnne and dropped some in my purse.

Maggie unwrapped hers and popped it into her mouth. "Now I understand why you carried that big bag."

Lumley tapped her on the shoulder. "May I have this dance?" She looked from me to LeeAnne.

LeeAnne shooed them off. "You two go have a good time. I'm going to mingle and run interference. Some of the ladies are waiting for a chance to swoop in and claim a dance with you, El."

Maggie and Lumley waltzed away; LeeAnne glided around the room and engaged people in conversation. I kept a vigil on the food table.

Most of the men sat on one side of the room, the women on the other, as at a proper ball, where the ladies wait for the gentlemen to make the first move. Annie encouraged some to meet on the dance floor but, for the most part, they all sat and enjoyed the music, or congregated with me around the food.

I kept Rick Garcon' Garrison busy refilling the sandwich and hors d'oeuvre platters. He ran back and forth casting furtive looks around the room as if irritated that his food supplies kept disappearing. A couple of times I caught sight of him in conversation with Annie, heads together, Annie holding his arm in a death grip, or pointing to one of the geriatric crowd. What could they possibly be discussing? I tried to listen, but couldn't make out

133

a word over the din of the music and mumbles of the crowd. She was probably upset that he couldn't keep the food table properly filled. Ah well, not my problem, I thought as I filled my plate for a third time and headed for the punch bowl where Wally Cox stood, smiling at me.

I stopped short of the punch bowl and, instead, concentrated on daintily scarfing down my food. A commotion drew my gaze. A young couple burst through the door, cameras flashing. I turned to Wally Cox. "Annie must have engaged the high school photography department for the shindig."

He leaned closer to me than was comfortable. "I don't think so. Take another look."

I watched the dashing young man in his tuxedo charm the ladies as he waltzed them around the floor and posed small groups for photos. His date was equally stunning in a formal of glittering gold; her long, dark hair framed her face and accentuated her large golden-hazel eyes.

Hazel eyes? Lights flashed in my brain. My hand went to my mouth and I gasped. "Omigod, it's the Cunninghams!"

Wally grinned. "Got it in one try."

"Frankie's transformation is amazing. Where are the business suit and large-rimmed glasses? And her hair isn't pulled into that tight French knot."

Wally nodded. "It seems as though our straight-laced all-business woman has morphed into Miss America."

I blinked and stared as I watched them circle the group like sleazy politicians, mingling with the crowd like they belonged there.

I took a bite of ham and cheese croissant, nudged Wally and

pointed across the room. "I think they've been found out. Look, Ora is pushing everyone out of the way to be at the head of the line for Jamie's time and attention."

Wally poured two cups of punch and handed one to me. "Mrs. Cunningham doesn't seem to mind. I guess she figures Ora and her crowd aren't much of a threat."

Frankie ignored Ora and circled the room with smiles and hugs for everyone.

Wally excused himself. "I think I'll go say hello to some folks— unless you would like this dance."

I held up my plate. "No thanks. I promised the next dance to this plate of food. Besides, I don't waltz."

As the pair approached the snack table from opposite sides of the room, Frankie veered around me and held out her hand to her husband.

"Ah, there you are, dear. Could I have the next dance?" They strolled away, Jamie's bones tapping, at least in my imagination, to the beat of some song about Paris.

Wally Cox kept popping up around me all evening. He was nicely dressed, not in a tux like Lumley, but a dress suit, white shirt with French cuffs, and the ever-present bow tie—this one in basic black. I couldn't dodge him completely, but managed to avoid dancing with him except for one rather bouncy number where I could hold him at arm's length. The thought of the man's head resting on my chest for a slow dance was less than appealing. However, his company that evening, on and off the dance floor, wasn't entirely annoying.

The bash broke up about nine o'clock, a late night for some of our geriatric crowd. Everyone thanked Annie and the

Cunninghams for the lovely party. Lumley escorted Maggie home, and I avoided Wally for fear he'd offer to walk me to my door. Instead, I crossed the room and grabbed LeeAnne's arm. "Come on," I said, "let me walk you home."

We all headed back to our apartments, well fed and well exercised, ready for a good night's sleep.

Saturday afternoon the Tricycle Girls got together to rehash the previous evening's events. In fact, groups all around the place met to discuss the Spring Fling. The hot topics in my living room were the transformation of Frankie and Jamie and the amount of jewels in view at the shindig.

"Frankie looked and acted more relaxed and amiable than I have ever seen her," said LeeAnne.

Maggie passed her the plate of cheese and crackers. "Yes, she really is lovely with her hair out of that severe hair style and without glasses. No one recognized her or Jamie at first."

"Humph," I snorted. "A couple of wolves wandering around in sheep's clothing."

"Well," said LeeAnne as she nibbled on a piece of cheese, "if they were looking for something to steal, the ladies sure gave them an eyeful. I swear some of them packed on everything in their jewelry boxes."

I nodded as I grabbed a pepper jack square and a cracker from the plate. "Did you see Kate McGinnis? She hovered around the ladies and asked loads of questions."

Maggie spoke up. "Yes, I did. What was that all about?"

I finished munching my cracker and brushed crumbs off my hands and lips. "I think she still wants to organize her 'Genealogy

Through Jewels' club. She had me post an article for the paper a few weeks ago but no one took much interest." I picked up another piece of cheese. "I guess the massive display of jewelry last night sent her head spinning. I'm surprised she didn't drag out the jeweler's loop or the 'history of jewels' manuals. It's possible she drummed up some business. And if not, it sure wasn't for lack of trying."

"Good for her," said LeeAnne. "That shows an entrepreneurial spirit. Everyone should stretch the limits of their abilities, especially we senior citizens."

"Speaking of stretching the abilities of seniors," I said, "did you see Ora Price practically knock Kate over to get to Jamie Cunningham when he walked in?"

"Yes," said Maggie. "I noticed the commotion and saw Kate stagger. I thought for a moment she and Ora were going to come to blows."

"I saw that, too," nodded LeeAnne. "What was it all about?"

"It might require a referee if anyone gets between Ora and Jamie," I said. "I think she's got a crush on him. She gave Maggie and me the evil eye the day we went to interview him. She's very possessive of him, hangs around the office all the time—presents him with her craft items—offers him cookies from the snack tray." I raised my eyebrows, "I think, as my mother would say, she's set her cap for him. Frankie had better watch out."

We all had a good laugh and fell back into relaxed silence, breaking up our gathering in time for dinner. The Spring Fling had been a success; everyone's spirits were lighter at Golden Harvest.

We kept watch on the Cunninghams, and somewhat less on Annie, but things seemed to have come to a standstill in our investigation. As spring gave way to the heavy warm humidity of early summer we grew complacent. The klepto-prankster receded to the backs of our minds. About the time we decided the perpetrator had tired of his or her game of hide-and-seek, things began to disappear again, this time with a twist; there was an upgrade to the pieces taken! Three weeks after the Spring Fling, Rose's ruby ring was replaced with a crystal bell. The place buzzed with excitement—the game was back on!

Chapter 21

It's All In the Game

And the 'game' continued. On the following Monday Gladys Martin found a Little Golden Book on her dressing table. Further inspection revealed her gold necklace and earrings had disappeared. Everywhere people gathered, a din like swarms of bees could be heard, everyone speculating who would be next, what the 'prize' would be, and where the pieces would eventually turn up.

I called LeeAnne and Maggie to my apartment to discuss the current situation. "Since you two socialize more than I do, you should pass the word around to all the 'chosen ones' that we are investigating the case and would appreciate it if they would bring their exchanged items to my apartment."

"Good idea," agreed LeeAnne. "That way we can check them out and perhaps pick up some clues. Maybe it will upset the perpetrator's plan."

Maggie scoffed. "What plan? We don't even know if there is a plan, let alone what it might be."

"That's true," said LeeAnne. "No one has bothered to file a stolen property report because they still believe we are in the midst of another scavenger hunt."

We went together to talk to the folks who had property taken. Some of them weren't too happy to turn over their trophies, but I assured them we would return all items when the game was over.

A few days later, all the residents received a flyer. Maggie brought hers with her to my apartment. "Have you checked your mail today?" She handed it to me. "Jamie Cunningham sent this out cautioning the residents to be sure to keep their doors locked. I guess that kind of eliminates him as a suspect."

"Either that, or he's trying to cloud the issue to make us believe he's not responsible."

LeeAnne showed up then and we studied the neat stack of six 'prizes' so far collected. "What are the latest items?" she asked.

I pulled a candle out of my shoulder bag. "Well, besides the bell and the book, we have this candle that was left in Leonard Ashburry's apartment in place of his solid gold lighter." I laid it down and added it to our inventory list. "There's also a clamshell ensconced in a clear polyethylene paperweight that replaced Pauline Finkle's pearls. Grace Lambert brought me a fan that had been left in place of her first edition Gone With The Wind, worth, she claimed, over $2,500."

"Ensconced in polyethylene?" Maggie laughed. "You're beginning to sound like a mad scientist or something."

"Merely attempting to be professional," I sniffed.

We labeled the 'prizes' with the owners' names as well as the values of the items taken as approximated by the residents estimates.

"Wow," said LeeAnne, "That's quite a haul!"

Maggie looked at her. "Not you too? Helen has you talking like some private detective. You're both taking this business too seriously. Next she'll have you reading those nursery rhyme mysteries she always has her nose in!"

LeeAnne blushed and nodded. "They're pretty good. Helen suggested, quite brilliantly I might add, they would hone my detecting skills."

Maggie groaned and collapsed into a chair. "What am I going to do with you two? It's bad enough Helen goes wandering around making accusations and building cases against everyone but the Pope..."

"The Pope doesn't live here," I reminded her.

"What?" She stared at me, wild blue eyes blazing.

I glanced down at our confiscated loot. "I'm only saying I'm sure the thief is somebody at Golden Harvest."

She shook her head like a freshly-bathed dog, rubbed her temples and glared at me. "You mean if the Pope lived here he would be a suspect?"

I shrugged. "Probably not. He's kind of old to be sneaking around the halls." I tried a smile in her direction.

"But," LeeAnne said, also with a smile, "he could easily get away with it. After all, who would suspect the Pope?"

Maggie moaned again, put her hands to her forehead and rested her elbows on the table. "What did I do to deserve this?"

She raised her head and shook her finger at us. "This is not some fairy tale, this is real life. And you two are not Nancy Drew and associate!"

I waddled over and patted her shoulder. "Come on, Mags, lighten up. You talk like we're in danger. No one has gotten hurt. No one is even very upset, because last time all the stuff showed back up. Maybe it is just a game to get these old fogies..."

She glared at me again.

I took a deep breath and started over. "…the *residents*," I continued, "to use some muscles besides their jaws and Bingo arms for a change."

LeeAnne patted Maggie's other shoulder. "Yes, perhaps that is true. You have to admit everyone is a lot more animated and observant lately."

Maggie sighed. She couldn't defeat both of us, even if she thought our logic was a bit skewed. She looked up at me. "Okay, I surrender. I'm outvoted."

"Not to mention out-weighed," I added.

LeeAnne picked up our list, ran her hand through her red hair. "So where do we go from here?"

I leafed through the Little Golden, *The Pokey Little Puppy*, one of my children's favorites, and said, "My money is still on the Cunninghams."

Maggie held up the flyer. "Don't you think it's strange that Jamie would issue a statement about keeping our doors locked if he is, in fact, the thief?"

I shook my head. "Not if he wants to keep suspicion away from himself. He is the so-called administrator. If he can't get people to file stolen property reports, he has to make the appearance of doing something."

I'm not so sure," said LeeAnne. "I'm not as convinced as you that the Cunninghams are behind this. Just because they took your friend's job doesn't mean they are criminals."

"Fine," I huffed. "Who else do you have in mind?"

She said slowly, "How about Kate McGinnis? She seems to have an almost obsessive curiosity about everyone's jewelry."

We considered that while we drank our tea. I hated to admit she had a point; all my energy had been expended on proving the cadaverous Jamie and his cat-wife had marched in to pillage our community. But what if I was *wrong*? The word stuck in my throat and nearly gagged me.

Finally, Maggie spoke up. "Kate McGinnis does like jewelry, but I don't think she's conniving enough to have put together this elaborate scheme. And her husband certainly doesn't seem to be the type. I've watched them around the place and they hardly speak to one another. It's like they float in different circles."

"Maybe," LeeAnne said, "they do that to throw us off track."

"It's possible," I agreed. "Let's add them to our list of suspects. Maggie, you can keep an eye on them. Anybody else come to mind?"

"If we are going to include improbable suspects, how about Annie?" suggested Maggie.

I choked on my tea. "Annie James, our camp coordinator? Roly-poly Annie?" The idea was, to me, past improbable and out into the field of impossible dreams. "If Annie is on the list, we might as well add Lennie the space cadet."

"Annie's title is, technically, Recreation Director," said Maggie with a smile. "And yes, I think she should be suspect." She waited for more argument but, hearing none, she continued. "Annie put together the Spring Fling. She knew everyone would bedeck themselves in all their finery to try to show one another up. It would be a good way to discover what valuables the residents have."

She added, quite proud of herself for the suggestion, "That way, Annie wouldn't have to rummage around in all the apartments to determine who would be worth robbing."

A nagging realization came to my mind. "The day she called me to her office about putting the article in the newsletter, she did tell me she liked nice jewelry but couldn't afford the real thing." Darn! Our list was getting out of hand.

"And," LeeAnne added, "maybe Lennie's space cadet persona is all an act. How better to avoid suspicion?"

I had to disagree about Lennie being a thief; no one is that good an actor. Nevertheless, I added him to the list—way at the bottom.

We couldn't come up with any other names so we broke up our meeting. As Maggie and LeeAnne were leaving I remembered something.

"Wait!" I shouted. I rifled through the papers on my desk and found what I was looking for. I handed them each a stack of cards. "Pass these out when you talk to people." I had printed full-color business cards for our new venture using my trusty computer and printer. The inscription, printed over a background of three figures on a tricycle caused them both to laugh.

Maggie read aloud: "HML Pedal Power—Healthy, Mature Ladies—Helen Patterson, Maggie Taylor, LeeAnne Warner—Tricycle Girls Investigation/Consultation"

She turned the card over. On the flip side, I had placed my phone number, and the words—No Job Too Small.

"Helen, these are very clever. Using our initials was a nice touch. Does that mean you are the healthy one, I'm mature and LeeAnne is the lady of our trio?"

"Yeah, although the H could also stand for Hefty."

"I'm glad you went with Healthy. But you put your phone

number on them. Do you think that's wise? You may get some crazy calls."

I shrugged. "How else would people get in touch with us?"

"Helen's right, Maggie," said LeeAnne. "Everyone here knows how to reach her anyway, so it's really no big deal.

"My favorite part is the tricycle built-for-three logo. I never noticed before how patriotic we are."

Maggie and I both stared at her.

She held out the card and pointed to the figures. "See, there's you in front, Helen, with your white hair. Maggie is hanging on the right side holding onto her blue-do, and that figure with her red hair flying is obviously supposed to represent me. Red, white and blue. All we need is a flag or a couple of sparklers to make us look really crazed!"

Maggie muttered, "This whole idea is a little crazed, if you ask me. Suddenly I'm getting a very bad feeling about this whole mess. Perhaps we should back off. I think we should convince the people who have been robbed to go to the police."

I patted Maggie's arm. "Jamie already tried to get them to file reports and they refused. What are you going to tell them that will make them change their minds?"

She chewed on her lower lip. "I don't know. I guess you're right, but let's be very careful, girls."

I practically shoved them out the door. "You worry too much. Playing detective is harmless fun. We aren't dealing with Jack-the-Ripper here. It's probably some senile old geezer—how fast can he run?"

Maggie squared off in front of me, and I had to come to a halt or barrel over her. "So you have decided the Cunninghams are innocent?" she asked.

I looked down at the toes of my worn sneakers and mumbled, "It's possible. I'm weighing my options. LeeAnne had a point."

"What point was that?" LeeAnne asked.

I looked at her. "There may be other people involved in the heists."

Maggie shook her head. "Honestly, Helen, your vocabulary is beginning to sound more and more like a Mickey Spillane novel!"

I took her by the shoulders and turned her around. "Thank you! This is the most fun I've had since I moved here. Now off with you. I'm going to put some of these business cards in the library."

"Good idea," said LeeAnne. "And you could post one on the bulletin board beside the events calendar."

Maggie groaned. "Don't encourage her, LeeAnne." But I noticed she smiled when she said it.

Two days later I found a business envelope on the floor inside my door. I laboriously bent down to pick it up. On the outside, in letters obviously cut at random from a magazine, was my name. I opened it and unfolded the single page note. In the same cutout letters as were on the envelope was a short but sinister message: PLAY THE GAME AT YOUR OWN RISK.

One of my new business cards floated to the floor, as did the note when it fell from my trembling hands.

Chapter 22

In a Quadricycle Built for Three

On rubbery legs I staggered to the phone to call Maggie, but after punching in half the numbers, I slammed the receiver down. I would *not* buckle under to that coward's threat! Besides, the revelation would add fuel to the fire of Maggie's fears. I repeated that out loud—add fuel to the fire of her fears. It had a nice ring to it, I liked the alliteration, and saying it aloud calmed me somewhat. I stomped back across the room, snatched up the note and crammed it into my legal pad. Not a good place, I decided. I found an unused manila folder and placed the offending threat inside, added copies of all my notes on our case that I had recently typed into my computer. I searched for a protected hiding place and finally filed the whole thing securely between my mattress and box springs in good gumshoe fashion.

What, exactly, had we done to cause the perp to threaten me? We must be closer to the truth than I realized. We were making him—or them—very nervous. I checked my lists of facts and suspects in hopes that something would jump out at me. Unfortunately, the only thing that jumped was me when someone knocked on my door. I cautiously opened it a crack and saw the beaming faces and coordinating outfits of my partners-against-crime.

"You look surprised to see us," said Maggie.

"And you two look like the Bobbsey Twins."

Maggie flashed me an indulgent smile. "Are you ready to go?"

"Go where?"

LeeAnne nudged her smiling accomplice. "See, Maggie. I told you we should call and remind her."

"Remind me about what? Am I missing something? It can't be Bingo, you know better than to subject me to that."

Maggie pushed her way into the room. "Did you forget we're going into town? LeeAnne's new car just arrived and we are going shopping and to lunch."

"Right, shopping and lunch," I said. "Of course I didn't forget. I've been organizing my notes and the time got away from me." Actually I had forgotten, but there was no need to tell them that.

Having someone with a car would be convenient. Neither Maggie nor I had brought vehicles with us to the place, even though it was allowed. I had used public transportation for years and the bus station was close. Besides, Golden Harvest had a van and driver that took residents on outings once or twice a week. I had always been a less than excellent driver, and had limited my infrequent automotive outings to places where there were curbs to guide me. At least that was the consensus of my children. They all claimed lasting scars from the traumas of being transported by me in their formative years to various games and events. They swore that when forced to operate a vehicle I would place my right tire against the curb like a slot car on a track and manage to get where I needed to be. Like the delivery people in those brown trucks, I only made right turns, and when the curbs stopped so did I. None of my children would ever change their stories, and at least one claimed to have been forced into therapy because of my driving. The ingrates!

I never got a ticket (that I wasn't able to erase by taking defensive driving) or had my name on a warrant for my arrest. That's more than some of them could say.

I gathered my shoulder bag and followed my friends out the door and into the parking lot.

"How's your driving record?" I asked LeeAnne.

"Never had a ticket," she said proudly.

"Me either," I said with a smile.

LeeAnne's car was a luxurious, top of the line Chrysler. I peered into the depths of the metallic blue paint job. The sensation was like diving into the blue-black ocean. I took a deep breath as I felt it draw me to the edge.

LeeAnne sensed my awe and held out the keys. "Would you like to drive?"

"NO!" screamed Maggie. She bolted in front of me, grabbed the dangling ring from LeeAnne's grasp and knocked her purse to the ground in the process.

As they bent to scoop up the contents, LeeAnne said, "Sorry, Maggie. Did you want to drive?"

Maggie chased a tube of lipstick under the car. "No, and I'm sorry I made such a fuss."

"Fuss?" I said. "I thought we were in grave danger the way you screamed."

"We would be with you behind the wheel," she said.

LeeAnne passed her a questioning look, so Maggie proceeded

to grace us with a list of the alleged details of my perilous past driving record as told by my offspring.

"They exaggerated. I wasn't that bad!" I huffed.

Maggie placed her hands on her hips. "Then why does Emily get a nervous tic in her right eye every time the subject comes up? And why did your kids get rid of your old clunker as soon as they had an excuse? And don't forget, I was with you when that guy at the tire place asked how all the rubber got rubbed off the edge of your passenger-side tires. He said the rims were more worn than the treads." By this time she was nearly in tears, she was laughing so hard.

"Is that true, Helen?" LeeAnne unlocked the doors and slid behind the wheel.

"I get to ride shotgun," I said, as I plopped into the passenger seat and slammed my door, ignoring both her question and Maggie's choked laughter.

"Nice car," I said as I pulled the seatbelt around my girth.

"Thanks." LeeAnne patted the dashboard before turning the key in the ignition. "Now the Tricycle Girls have wheels."

Maggie had finally stopped her cackling and spoke up from the backseat. "Technically, your car has four wheels. Maybe we should rename ourselves the Quadricycle Girls." With that she again burst into hysterical laughter.

I turned my head to glare at her. "You're a real comedian today."

She dug around in her purse looking for something—maybe her new book of snappy one-liners about my lack of driving skills. "Oh, Helen," she snickered, "don't be such a grouch. I was only teasing." She smiled at me. "Do you have a tissue? My eyes are watering and I can't find mine."

I handed her my pocket pack. "Serves you right for laughing at me."

Maggie lowered her gaze.

"Besides," I added, a half-smile turning up the corners of my mouth, "we can't change our name, I already made up the business cards."

"Right," she and LeeAnne said in unison. Not very convincingly, I might add.

"Where to, girls?" asked LeeAnne as she turned onto the main road and headed toward town. "I'm new to the area. Who's going to navigate?"

I crossed my arms in front of me. "Guess I will, since I'm not allowed to actually drive. It's nearly lunchtime. Shall we eat before we shop?"

They agreed that was a good idea so I told LeeAnne to turn right at the second light in town.

After she made the turn I said, "Now make another right two blocks down."

LeeAnne followed my directions.

"When we get to Elm, make another right. The Downtown Café is at the end of the block."

"On the right," added Maggie. "See, LeeAnne, that proves my point. Helen only makes right turns."

I twisted my neck toward the back seat. "Don't you dare start laughing again, Maggie Taylor, or I will…"

She bit her lip to hold back a snicker. "Or you will what?"

"I will not let you order pie!" I couldn't hold back any longer, and we all laughed so hard we almost missed the last available parking spot close to the café.

We were seated in what was once a display window of the quaint eating establishment. The storefront had originally been a small shop; now tables had replaced window dressing, and customers served as living mannequins.

"Are we supposed to wave and smile, or sit very still?" asked LeeAnne. "I feel like I'm on display."

I picked up my menu, even though I already knew I was going to order my usual spinach wrap and creamed potato bisque. "You can wave if you want to, but I'm here to eat, not entertain the pedestrians."

LeeAnne and Maggie finally settled on turkey clubs and minestrone soup. The Downtown Café also boasts the most delicious iced blackberry herbal tea in the civilized world, so we all sipped cold tea served in frosty crystal glasses while Maggie gave LeeAnne a seated guided tour of the town. "In the 1930's and '40's, the building next door to the café was a department store. Now it has been refurbished and houses three floors of antiques."

LeeAnne perked up at that. "Are there any other antique shops in town? I love browsing around old things."

"Oh, yes," said Maggie, "I know of several good places we could check out. Right, Helen?"

I stopped eating long enough to answer. "Yeah, a trio of old things looking at old things. Great fun!"

Maggie leaned closer and stage-whispered to LeeAnne, "Helen thinks antiques are nothing more than old stuff people don't want any more, and are trying to pawn off on someone else for an exorbitant price."

LeeAnne nodded. "In some cases that's true. But I get

nostalgic when I see a dish or toy or something I remember from my childhood."

Maggie patted her hand. "We'll take a day soon and go antiquing."

I pointed my soupspoon in her direction. "Not today, though. We came to town to clothes shop!"

Maggie smiled. "I wouldn't miss a trip that gets you into a clothing store."

She continued to fill LeeAnne in on some of the historic buildings in town, pointing across the street. "That's the bank over there, built by Andrew Settlemeyer in 1890. It's still owned and operated by the Settlemeyer family."

As she spoke, three familiar-looking people exited the building. I squinted into the bright light shining through the window. "Isn't that the Cunninghams?"

"Yes, and that's Elsworth Lumley with them," said LeeAnne. "They seem to be having a serious conversation. I wonder what that's all about?"

I slapped my hand on the table so hard the plates jumped. "I knew he was mixed up in this mess!" Startled by the noise, several of the other restaurant patrons glanced at us.

Maggie grabbed my arm. "Helen, don't start that nonsense again!" Her voice issued a warning, but her eyes showed hurt and confusion.

"Maybe it's nothing," said LeeAnne. "They probably saw each other in the bank, and Elsworth is only being polite."

"Humph!" I said. "Looks like more than polite conversation to me."

Maggie's silent stare shut me up, and I attempted to change

153

the subject. "Maybe I will look at some of those Capri pants you two like so much." That got their attention.

"Really, Helen?" said LeeAnne. "How many right turns to get to the department store?"

I pointed my fork at her. "Don't you start; and, to answer your question, it's only a couple of blocks from here. We could walk that far."

"Yes, but then we would have to carry all our packages back to the car," said Maggie.

I didn't plan on buying that much stuff, but our driver said, "Okay, it's settled. We take the car."

After a delicious dessert of apple pie a la mode all around, we headed toward the department store. Some of those new mega-stores had gone up on the other side of town, but Maggie and I preferred to shop the old, established places in downtown. We knew the proprietors, and somebody had to take a stand against the conglomerates squashing all the small businesses across America.

Happy's Pawn Shop seemed to be doing a booming business as we passed by and parked two doors down in front of Mitchell's Millinery. Just as we got to the door of Mitchell's, I saw Annie James duck into the pawn shop. The canvas bag she carried must have been loaded down the way her shoulder sagged as she walked. I doubted it was filled with cosmetics. Neither Maggie nor LeeAnne saw her, and both were skeptical when I mentioned seeing Annie with 'the loot'.

"People pawn stuff all the time," Maggie said. "Maybe she needed some extra money. I'm sure she doesn't make a lot as our recreation director."

"Yeah," I said. "Or she could be pawning the stuff she stole from the residents. She just went to the top of my list of suspects."

"Did you say she carried the bag as if it were heavy?" asked LeeAnne.

"Yes, why?"

"Even if she put all the missing things in one bag, it shouldn't weigh a great deal."

She had a point, but I couldn't get Annie off my mind as we went about our shopping. Maggie and LeeAnne picked up some more spring fashions and I looked at, but didn't buy, some Capri pants. There was no way I could picture myself wearing an outfit that showcased my dimpled knees. The next time the van made a trip to Nifty Thrifty, I'd look for some good buys. I did pick up a pair of sandals though; I may buy recycled clothes, but I stop short of wearing someone else's shoes!

We were all exhausted by the time we got back to Golden Harvest, and headed to our respective apartments to freshen up before dinner. When I opened my door, my answering machine light was blinking. I pressed the button and a familiar voice filled the room. The ominous warning said, "Helen. Elsworth Lumley, here. I saw one of your business cards in the library. I must insist that you not pursue this missing jewelry business. You ladies are putting yourselves at risk. You need to stop this nonsense immediately!"

After the click at the end of his message, a tingle of fear ran up my spine. Elsworth Lumley replaced Annie at the top of my list.

Chapter 23

Three Blind Mice

We met that evening at the supper table, Maggie and LeeAnne wearing some of their new togs, me in my hibiscus outfit and my new sandals.

LeeAnne gave me the once-over, shook her napkin and laid it on her lap. "I guess our next shopping trip will have to be to Nifty Thrifty to get Helen some clothes."

Maggie nodded in agreement. "Good plan. You look nice, this evening, LeeAnne. I wish I could wear green. Those blended shades really go well with your red hair and accentuate your lovely green eyes."

"Thank you, Maggie, you look nice, too. But there's no reason why you can't wear green."

I stirred the sugar in my tea and pointed the spoon at Maggie's head. "Ha! Not unless she dyes her hair a different shade of blue."

Maggie cocked the aforementioned blue locks in my direction but addressed our dinner companion. "Oh oh. We're about to be the recipients of Mizz Helen's fashion advice." She looked at me. "What is it this time, Helen? Another of your mother's fashion faux pas?"

I shrugged, took a sip of my tea and reached for two more packets of sugar.

Maggie again spoke to LeeAnne. "Helen's mother and all her friends used to rake the ladies they considered outsiders over the coals for their style blunders." She smiled in my direction and patted my hand. "The whole process created in Helen a very warped picture of proper dress etiquette."

I nodded. "That's right. But I never did find that fashion bible they constantly referred to."

LeeAnne said, "You mean the one that states things like 'Thou shalt not wear white before Easter or after Labor Day?'"

I tilted my glass toward her. "Exactly. Where do they keep that book, anyway?"

She sipped her totally unsweetened tea. "I don't know; but I do know the rules used to be very strictly enforced on most fashion matters." She gave me that knowing look. "No wonder you fight being fashion conscious if you were forcibly subjected to that. I take it you didn't submit graciously."

"Hah!" Maggie said. "Helen didn't submit at all. She always looked like a street urchin."

I sighed and flashed LeeAnne a poor-pitiful-me smile. "It's true. When Mama had guests for tea she only let me come into the house when Maggie was with me, and then she pretended Maggie was her child and I was the ragamuffin friend." I sighed again for effect.

LeeAnne had a mouthful of tea and nearly showered us all when she laughed.

Maggie patted my hand. "Po-oo-or little Helen."

I pulled my hand away. "You know better than anyone,

Maggie Taylor, there was never anything little about me."

I addressed our dinner partner. "My mother said no one in her linage had ever been as large and gangly as I turned out; and my father was not much better. He'd shake his head and say, "Well, don't blame me!""

Maggie shook her head. "It wasn't that bad, Helen. Most of that recollection is only in your own mind. You have always been independent and headstrong. You never fit into that box your mother had planned for you—the sweet, dainty child with curly locks and frilly dresses. She always wondered where she went wrong."

"Poor Mama," I sighed. "I guess I was a disappointment to everyone."

"Not to us!" LeeAnne and Maggie said in unison. We raised our glasses and LeeAnne toasted, "To the Tricycle Girls." We touched rims and swallowed hearty gulps of our tea.

"So," said LeeAnne, after the toast, "did anyone besides me sneak a nap after our shopping trip?"

"I sat down and put my feet up," said Maggie. "Elsworth called to say hi and we talked for a while."

"He's so sweet," cooed LeeAnne. "What else did he say, or is it none of my business?" she teased.

"He *is* sweet," agreed Maggie. "He said he was concerned about our investigation of the missing valuables."

"Uh huh," I muttered. "What did you tell him?"

"I told him exactly what you told me, Helen—that it's a harmless mental exercise like working a logic puzzle. We are only filling in some blanks. No one is getting hurt by our actions."

I leaned forward and rested my arms on the table. "Good for

you! And what did Lumley have to say about that?"

Maggie flashed one of those saccharine-sweet, adolescent smiles. "He said to be very careful, that he is concerned for my welfare."

"Humph! I bet he is."

LeeAnne and Maggie exchanged sidelong glances. "What is that supposed to mean?" Maggie asked. "Don't tell me you still suspect El of any wrongdoing?"

I folded my arms loosely across my chest. "I don't mean anything by it, except I don't think Elsworth Lumley is who he claims to be. I got…" I clamped my lips shut. No way was I going to tell Maggie about Lumley's threatening message on my answering machine. Not yet, anyway. She would do one of two things: take his side and swear I was over-exaggerating, or get mad at me. On second thought, she would probably do both; I didn't want that. I needed her close so I could keep an eye on her, for her own safety. I would have to watch Lumley too, although his safety would only be an issue if he messed with my friends.

The two of them looked at me quizzically. "You got *what*, Helen?" LeeAnne finally asked.

"I got to looking at my notes," I stammered, "and everything seems to lead back to him and the Cunninghams."

"That's because you have a one-track mind." Maggie waved a finger at me. "You are just like that terrier I had as a child. Do you remember her?"

I had to reach way back into long-term memory, but finally it came to me. "You mean Bootsie?"

"Yes, Bootsie." She spoke to LeeAnne by way of explanation. "My dad trained Bootsie to chase mice, and every time he would point and shout, "Mouse!" she would be off like a shot. She would root around all day searching for would-be rodents. One day she chased so long and hard she dropped dead of a heart attack."

"She was persistent, wasn't she?" I had to smile thinking about that dog tearing around behind the curtains, under the sofa, short legs flying. Her toenails clip-clip-clipped on the linoleum, tongue lolled out, and her eyes glazed over as she pursued her prey, real or imagined.

"I'm not *that* bad. And she probably dropped dead because she was old."

Maggie's blue eyes stared directly into mine, her arms crossed defiantly across her chest. "You *are* that bad, Helen. And, I might add, you are no youngster yourself. I don't want to be worried about your blood pressure sky-rocketing you into oblivion," she relaxed and smiled, "right along with your mind."

"Ha ha," I said. "Thanks for your concern. I will take it under advisement." It was our stock answer to end an altercation when one of us had made a logical argument for a truce.

Maggie leaned toward LeeAnne, who had maintained silence throughout our tirade. "Sorry about that outburst, dear. Helen and I have been going on like this for years. You'll get used to it after a while."

We eyed each other and said, in unison, "I did!"

At that, we all laughed so hard the other diners cast strange glances in the direction of our table. We didn't care; all was well again with the Tricycle Girls.

Chapter 24

Yes! We Have Likely Suspects

We finished our dinner with no more incidents—as in, no more arguments and no spilled drinks; and we toasted our evening as a success with our last sips of tea.

As we rose to leave, LeeAnne asked, "Is everyone game to take Helen to Nifty Thrifty tomorrow?"

"Sounds good to me," agreed Maggie.

They turned to me for affirmation.

"You two are awfully anxious to redesign my wardrobe," I said. "But I'm always up for the Nifty Thrifty. Just don't expect me to buy any of those short pants!"

My two companions nodded. "Deal!" We headed in separate directions; me to the library, LeeAnne to her apartment, and Maggie suspiciously quiet about her evening plans.

Later, in my apartment, my eyes and nose both started running, and I feared I was catching an early summer cold. I dosed myself with decongestants and went to bed. In my antihistamine-induced dreams I had the pointed nose of a small terrier, and I was running around on short legs chasing a rodent with a head that bore the likeness of Elsworth Lumley. After a seemingly endless pursuit, the rodent and I both collapsed. He stared at me with his beady steel gray eyes and yipped, "Tell Maggie to be careful."

I woke up exhausted and with sore leg muscles. I pulled my tired, achy body out of bed and ran my hands through my tousled hair. "Wow! That's the last time I'm taking those decongestants!"

I showered and dressed and after breakfast we headed out the door for our "real" shopping excursion. The reason for my nighttime sniffles became apparent. During the night clouds of pine pollen had snowed down on us. The whole place was covered with a thin layer of yellow pine 'snow'. LeeAnne's car, deep blue yesterday, was covered, as was everything else in sight.

I sneezed. "Ah, Georgia spring is definitely in the air. Guess we will have to hit the carwash sometime today."

"There's a full-service one two doors down from the thrift store," said Maggie. "Maybe we can drop it off while we shop." She took LeeAnne's arm. "And there are two antique shops within walking distance. If we finish at Nifty Thrifty before the car gets done, we can browse for a while."

"You're determined to get me into those antique places, aren't you?" I groused.

"There's also a restaurant within walking distance," she said, taking my arm with her free hand. We waddled unsteadily down the sidewalk to the pollen-drenched car and climbed in, with me again riding shotgun.

LeeAnne buckled herself in, turned the key in the ignition, and flipped the wipers on to clear the yellow fluff from the window. "What is this yellow stuff, and how long will it last? It's playing havoc with my sinuses, not to mention the mess it made on my car!"

I jerked my head in her direction and Maggie leaned forward

162

from her seat in the back. We had both been born and raised in Georgia, and assumed all other intelligent people, especially those we had affection for, were natives as well. It never occurred to us that, although our new friend admitted to a lifetime of travel, she might not be "one of us".

"It's pine pollen. Where are you from?" I blurted out.

She gave me a quick glance before returning her eyes to the road. "I was born in upstate New York, but have, as I told you, lived in lots of places—never in a place where yellow snow fell in the spring, though. The snow in the north turns yellow for a different reason." She laughed at her joke.

Maggie grabbed the back of my seat and pulled herself farther forward behind me. "How did you ever end up in Loblolly?"

LeeAnne eyed Maggie through the rearview mirror. "When Charlie retired we bought a place in Florida. I had become enamored of raising orchids, and Charlie, bless his heart, had read that Florida was a great place to grow them." She sighed, brushed a hand across her eyes and through her immaculately groomed red hair. Her face took on that far-away look reserved for special memories, the birth of a first-born child, and lost loves.

"Charlie sounds like a peach," Maggie finally said.

"Yes, he was." LeeAnne chuckled. "He indulged me terribly; I was like a spoiled child. It got to a point where I was afraid to say I liked something for fear he would go out and buy it for me."

"Sounds to me like you hit the mother lode with that man," I said with awe—and just a teeny note of jealousy.

LeeAnne shrugged. "I guess. But I never needed any of those things. Just knowing he loved me was enough." She cleared her throat and swallowed hard. "But you were inquiring how I ended up at Golden Harvest. After Charlie died, I needed to make some changes in my life. He had provided for my security, but I realized I couldn't stay in that house with all those memories."

Maggie patted her shoulder. "I certainly understand. I experienced the same emotions after my Bill passed away."

LeeAnne nodded and continued, never taking her eyes off the road, but occasionally glancing in the rearview mirror to make eye contact with Maggie. "You may think this a silly way to decide one's future, but I got information on all the retirement homes in a four state area. I read all the brochures and placed the business cards of the ones that sounded promising into a bowl. I picked out three at random, checked them out, and 'voila', here I am."

"You mean the Tricycle Girls got our third wheel by the luck of the draw?" I asked with a grin.

LeeAnne smiled back. "Yup. That's about it."

"And a wonderfully lucky draw for us," said Maggie, always ready with the right thing to say.

LeeAnne turned to me. "Okay, Ms. Navigator, where do we make our first right turn?"

"I'm never going to live that down, am I?"

Maggie settled back into her non-navigator back seat. "Nope, not in this lifetime."

"Fine, then, make a right on Main—that's two stoplights down. Go four blocks and make another right."

We passed the grand old courthouse that, Maggie informed LeeAnne, had been around since 1898. If she couldn't be navigator, she could be an excellent tour guide. The old granite-faced building stood tall and majestic, fresh from its million-dollar makeover.

"If someone spent a million dollars on me, I'd be majestic too," I grumbled.

"Don't mind Helen, LeeAnne; she thinks the county would have been better served by building sanctuaries for important things—like terns or alligators."

"Yeah, unlike politicians, you always know the agenda of an alligator." I pointed out the window. "This is it."

We dropped the car off to be spruced up and walked two doors down to the Nifty Thrifty, where I picked out a navy blue blazer and two lightweight, permanent-press blouses. I was browsing in the back corner, where all the seriously marked-down items were hidden, when Maggie rushed up behind me.

"Here, Helen, try these on. They're perfect for you!"

I turned to see what had her so excited. She was holding what appeared to be a large, dark blue cotton skirt. The waist was elastic, which was in its favor. "I don't need a skirt," I told her.

"But it's not a skirt." She grabbed one leg of the things and pulled it up. "See? I think they're called Gaucho pants. And in your size, too!"

So, despite my determination to keep my richly dimpled knees covered, and my argument that I was not a gaucho, I ended up purchasing a pair of short pants. Maggie and LeeAnne grinned perversely as we trudged back to pick up the car.

My curiosity had got the best of me, and I asked LeeAnne to stop by the pawn shop. I had known Bennett Royal, the owner, all his life. He and my son, Aaron, ran around together when they were kids. That is, until my wayward son decided to become an aerialist. Bennett used to call me Mama Patterson or Mama P, and he spent so much time at my house I threatened to claim him as a deduction on my income taxes. I knew things about him even his own mother didn't know.

Unfortunately, he refused to give me any information about Annie or what she had pawned. "I'm sorry, Mama Patterson, but I am legally bound by the Privacy Act."

I leaned on the glass counter and gave him my fiercest motherly frown. "Does your mother know about you and the pot-smoking incident?"

He gulped and held up his hands in protest. "No Mama P. But even if you told her—which I hope you won't—I can't divulge information about a customer. If you feel this lady has stolen something from you, you could go to the police and file a report. Do you want to do that?"

"No, no. Thanks anyway, Bennett. Sorry to bother you. Nice seeing you again."

He visibly relaxed. "You too, Mama Patterson. Tell Aaron 'Hi' when you see him. Is he still trying to climb to the top of the world?"

I shook my head. "Afraid so. Tell your mother hello."

As I reached the door I turned and smiled. "I won't tell her about the pot."

He let out a sigh of relief, and waved. "Thanks."

I climbed back in the car. "No luck," I reported. "Bennett gave me some story about the Privacy Act."

As we pulled out onto the street, Maggie pointed. "Look there. Isn't that Rick Garrison walking into the pawn shop?"

"It certainly is!" I said. "And the bag he has slung over his shoulder looks a lot like the one Annie was carrying yesterday."

We looked at each other. "Annie and Rick?" we all said at once.

Chapter 25

Loves Me, Loves Me Not

Our next stop was the Wheel House Restaurant for lunch. The place had been in business, of one sort or another, since the 1870's. LeeAnne, with Maggie again as tour guide, took in all the sketches and photos that traced the history of the establishment. In the 1800's, the building served as a livery stable and wagon repair—one of those ancestors of the modern-day vehicle repair shops—back when Fix-A-Flat had a much different meaning, a tune up involved something different than changing spark plugs, and the shoe store catered to the four-footed variety. The place had also included an inn for people passing through town, and eventually expanded services to include meals for the wayfaring travelers. At one period in its history the Wheel House sported a gentlemen's club on its upper floor, where men could gather to smoke cigars and partake of the "spirits". Rumor has it they partook of other things as well but, being the gentlemen they were, they didn't tell, so it's all lost in history or left to the imagination.

Tintype photographs of dapper mustached men in ill-fitting suits and jaunty derby hats lined the walls. The men in the photos congregated inside and outside the building, leaned against the hitching post, held the reins of anxious horses. Later pictures showed horseless carriages mingling with the wagons, fewer men with hairy faces. Finally, some ladies posed among the men, the gentlemen grasping their arms lest the fair sex get sucked into the bawdy atmosphere of the place. Even the more modern photos were in black and white in keeping with the décor.

As our heels tapped across the hardwood floors following the hostess to our table, LeeAnne commented, "I feel as though I've gone through a time-warp. The atmosphere almost screams hoop skirts and large-brimmed hats."

"And parasols," added Maggie.

To keep it real I said, "Yes, and if that were the case, three unescorted ladies in this den of iniquity in the 1800's could mean only one thing." I waggled my finger in front of them as we sat down, "We would be defined as 'working girls'. I don't know about you two, but that kind of work is way outside my choice as a job preference!" We all laughed in agreement to that and toasted the fact with the large glasses of iced tea the waitress had set in front of us.

LeeAnne pursed her lips after one swallow. "I forgot where I am. A special dispensation is required for unsweetened tea in this state."

That is not true of all southern restaurants, but in one like the Wheel House that serves up good old down home cooked meals, most of which come with grits, you must expect sweet tea. The menu includes such fare as chicken-fried steak, Bar-B-Que—pork, of course—fried okra, black-eyed peas, turnip greens and cornbread, as well as the aforementioned grits. What more could a southern appetite crave? Georgia Peach Cobbler, the special of the house, that's what! I may not be a gourmet cook, but I am a gourmet eater. I know good food when I eat it—and I am proud to say I can eat with the best of them!

LeeAnne requested and received, with recognition from the waitress that this one was definitely a foreigner, unsweetened tea. We checked our menus, ordered our bar-b-que and chatted while we waited. The conversation finally came around to Rick Garrison, his bag, and what it might contain.

"I'm almost positive that was the same bag Annie carried into the pawn shop yesterday," I said. "I sure would like to know what they have been disposing of."

LeeAnne raised her eyebrows. "Personally, I would like to know if they are a couple."

Maggie laid her napkin in her lap. "If not, it's not for lack of trying—at least on Annie's part. You can almost hear the sexual tension in the air when they are in the same room."

LeeAnne and I exchanged looks. Maggie had taken to reading historical romances lately, and those things had obviously affected her mind.

"Maggie," I said, "I don't think I have ever heard you utter the phrase 'sexual tension'. Is it those wild romances you have been reading or is the history of this bawdy establishment loosening your tongue?"

She blushed and coughed into her napkin. LeeAnne nudged my arm. "Sounds to me like Maggie might have a little sexual tension of her own going on, Helen."

I stared at her and she looked down at her hands. "Is that true, Mags? Are you getting serious about Lumley?"

She raised her head, tilted it to one side and stared as if focusing on an object across the room would help frame her answer. "I don't know about *serious*, but El and I enjoy each other's company very much." Her voice trailed away as though she was lost in thought.

LeeAnne and I leaned closer and said in unison, "AND?"

Maggie looked up, a smile playing at the corners of her mouth, "*And* he's a very good kisser." She sipped her tea and eyed us as we sat there with our mouths hanging open.

LeeAnne found her voice first. "Tell us more," she pleaded.

Maggie held up her hands in protest and said, "The topic is not open for discussion."

"You brought it up," I reminded her.

She set her glass on the table. "Yes, I did. And now I'm bringing it down. I'm afraid if I say anything I'll jinx the relationship. Things are fine right now, and I don't want to think about what ifs."

LeeAnne and I exchanged looks. Our friend was falling for Lumley. *What if* he didn't share her feelings? *What if* he was just passing time? Or worse, *what if* he was, as I suspected, mixed up in the awful mess at Golden Harvest? I'm not good at advice to the lovelorn, but I am smart enough to know there is no way to talk a person out of falling in love. I hoped Maggie knew what she was falling into. I would really have to keep an eye on things. Too bad the state had outlawed running ne'er-do-wells out of town on a rail. I couldn't think of anyone to help me carry out that sentence anyway. Tarring and feathering had also become a lost art— probably, I decided, because hot tar was awfully messy. Besides, where would I order a bucket of tar? I hadn't ever had an occasion to check the phone directory or the Internet for hot tar deliveries, but I hear you can buy most anything on the Internet. Maybe I'd check it out.

I awoke from my reverie to the insistent sound of Maggie's voice. "Helen, do you want dessert?"

"What?" I blinked and looked up at the waitress. "Of course. I've got to top my meal off with a bowl of peach cobbler." I glanced at my tablemates. "Aren't you two having anything?"

Maggie smiled. "We already ordered. You were concentrating so hard on something, I'm surprised you even know what you ate. What were you thinking about?"

I looked at my empty plate. The residual taste of bar-b-que lingered on my tongue and I was no longer hungry; but, for the life of me, I couldn't remember having eaten. I mentally kicked myself for wasting a good meal. It was all Elsworth Lumley's fault, him and his intentions toward my lifelong friend.

Since Maggie's romance was off limits, we discussed the possibility of Annie and Rick being a couple.

"I think it's sweet," said LeeAnne.

"You would," I huffed. "You're an incurable romantic."

Maggie lifted a spoonful of steaming peach cobbler to her mouth, "Yes Helen, and you are an incorrigible cynic. It seems to me, we have both sides of the scale here, you on one side, LeeAnne on the other."

"Really?" I asked. "So where does that put you?"

She blew on her spoonful of cobbler, "I," she said, "am the unwavering voice of reason in this little triad of ours."

I nearly choked on my dessert. LeeAnne laughed and said, "Actually, that's a fairly accurate description. That's why we work to well together; between us we have all the elements of good problem-solving—direction, emotion and logic." She raised her glass. "Let's toast to our success."

I touched glasses with them and added, "So far, we've done a lot more toasting this problem than solving it. We need more information. One of us needs to get closer to Annie."

Maggie spoke up. "I might have an idea. LeeAnne, does Janine still want you to help organize a talent show?"

She nodded, "Lord, yes. The woman is relentless. Why?"

Maggie dabbed her mouth with her napkin. "I thought that might be a way to get close to Annie. If you and Janine are working on a show involving the residents, Annie, as the recreation director, will have to get involved with all the programs and promotion—helping to set up times and places for auditions; you know, all the background work. That way, you can watch her and she won't suspect you have an ulterior motive."

LeeAnne groaned, but after considering the idea said, "It might be kind of fun. We could have singing and dancing, recitations; everyone has some talent." She grinned at Maggie, "Helen could do her stand-up comedy routine."

I shook my head, never raising my head from my bowl of peach cobbler. "Ha, ha. You can count me out. I'll be the audience. Besides, I have to report the big event for the Harvester. You two go ahead. I'm not making a fool of myself in front of everyone!"

I had to admit it wasn't a bad idea—Maggie's voice of reason had struck home again. We were so engrossed in discussing our plan none of us was aware another person had approached our table.

"Excuse me."

We all jumped at the voice and raised our heads to see its source. "I heard you talking about a talent show, and I would like to audition," the slight man stated.

LeeAnne smiled, Maggie elbowed me and I spoke. "Hello, Wally. What brings you to town?"

He pointed toward the remnants of our desserts. "Same thing that brought you lovely ladies here; this delicious cobbler. And, by the way, my name is actually Bernard—Bernie." He held out his hand to LeeAnne. "Let me introduce myself. Wally—a.k.a. Bernie—Cox."

LeeAnne returned the handshake. "Hello, Mr. Cox. I'm pleased to meet you. I've seen you around Golden Harvest, but haven't had a chance to learn everyone's names."

"Please call me Wally."

"Why Wally, if your name is Bernie?" I asked him.

His smile twinkled in his dark blue eyes. "I guess you could call it vanity, or desire for recognition. People used to tell me how much I looked like Mr. Peepers, so I decided to use it to my advantage." He stepped back and with a sweeping gesture said, "As you can plainly see, I don't have a whole lot going for me."

From my vantage point in a sitting position, I could see his face instead of the top of his head. He was kind of cute—in a myopic sort of way. I asked if he would like to join us, and Maggie and LeeAnne seconded the invitation. After he had seated himself between LeeAnne and me and put in his order for cobbler, I said, "So you want to be in the talent show?"

He managed a shy grin. "Yes, it sounds like fun."

LeeAnne folded her hands on the table and asked in her most serious directorial voice, "What is your talent," she smiled sweetly,

173

"besides imitating Mr. Peepers?"

He let out a hearty laugh. "I used to play tenor saxophone in a jazz ensemble. It was years ago, but I still get the old sax out of mothballs occasionally to keep it oiled up—and to see if I'm still in good enough shape to make music that doesn't call wild turkeys."

I smiled and nudged his arm. "I'm sure, Wally—or would you prefer Bernie? that you make beautiful music. I have always liked the sound of a saxophone."

He blushed. "You may call me Bernie, if you like. That's what my close friends call me."

"Bernie it is, then," said LeeAnne as she patted him on the back. "Helen will post an ad for open auditions when we get that far. Right now it's just an idea; I'm sure we'll have to get approval from the administrator first."

"Please come," added Maggie. "I'm sure you will be a wonderful asset to the show."

Bernie blushed again. We visited for a few more minutes while he ate his cobbler, then Maggie looked at her watch. "I hate to rush you girls, but I told El I'd stop by and drop off some books to him when we got back."

Bernie stood with us and we shook hands all around. He smiled broader and held onto my hand a bit longer than he did the others. His grip was firm and warm, but not clammy – a nice, steady hand. "Thanks for letting me join you for dessert, Helen." He nodded to Maggie and LeeAnne. "Ladies. I'll see you back at the Over-the-Hillton." He held the door for us as we exited the restaurant and headed for our respective vehicles.

Once safely inside the car, Maggie said, "LeeAnne, I think Bernie-Wally likes Helen."

LeeAnne nodded enthusiastically. "I think you're right. What about it, Helen?"

I blushed and shook my head. "I'm going to tell you what you told us, Maggie. The subject is not open for discussion. Besides, the man simply stopped by our table for dessert and to invite himself into the talent show." But on the way back home I thought about his sweet smiling eyes, his gentle laugh and his nice voice. I abruptly came back to my senses and considered the fact that when we were standing, my view would be of the top of his head and those smiling eyes would be focused on my chest. It would never work out!

Chapter 26

The Show Must Go On

The Cunningham's gave their approval for us to stage a show. We called a group meeting in LeeAnne's apartment so she could give us the low-down on what happened when she approached Janine about helping to organize the show. She reported that she had been met with a screeched "YES!", a bear hug, and much jumping up and down on the Snow Queen's part.

"I bet the woman dislodged a kidney in her exuberance," she said.

Maggie laughed and nodded in understanding. "Yours or hers?"

LeeAnne tucked a curl behind her ear. "Hers, I hope. But look at my hair! I had it pulled up this morning, and she jostled all the bobby pins out!"

I snorted. "That's just the beginning. By the time Janine's finished with you, you'll have bald spots from pulling out your hair in frustration."

Maggie shook her head in LeeAnne's direction. "Janine's not that bad; she's just stage-struck. This program will give her an outlet to showcase her talent."

I poured myself some more juice and asked if anyone else needed a refill before I asked, "What talent? Besides, as one of the organizers she should be excluded from performing. I, for one, don't want to hear her save Christmas again!"

LeeAnne popped a grape in her mouth and sipped her juice. "It's an open audition. That means anyone can try out, so I guess we can't exclude her."

"Okay," I said. "Do I get to be the deciding vote about Janine?"

My friends both looked at me. Finally, Maggie spoke, "I think we might need to get someone a bit more objective."

LeeAnne waved her hand in the air in dismissal of the subject. "We'll figure that out when and if the need arises." She pointed in Maggie's direction. "You're objective, perhaps you could be the third vote."

Maggie shook her blued, curly locks in dismissal. "No, no. If it came to that I would be forced to put her through, or she would claim Helen influenced my vote. I pass."

"We may not even have to make the decision," I said. "We've got to focus on the real reason we staged this thing, and that is to get close to Annie. Everything else is secondary."

We met later in the week in LeeAnne's apartment to tweak the wording on the notice for auditions. Finally, we were satisfied with its content. Maggie read:

"Attention, Residents: On June 7th at 2 o'clock p.m., open auditions for a talent show will be held in the dining/auditorium area. Come with your skits, recitations, instruments and/or music. The organizing committee of Annie James, Janine Hopgood and LeeAnne Warner will consider all acts, with final selection at the discretion of the committee.

Accompaniment will be provided by Rachel Miller for singers who bring sheet music."

We all nodded. "Sounds good," LeeAnne said. "Annie said we could use her office as the holding room for those trying out. Everyone can fill out a sign-up sheet and we'll call them in one at a time. That way everyone feels special, and no one has to perform in front of the other participants."

"Don't they know they'll be performing in front of everybody at the show?" I asked. "If they are that shy, they shouldn't be trying out."

"It's not that, Helen," LeeAnne explained. "This way, no one knows what anyone else is doing. It will be a big surprise the night of the show."

I pointed my gel pen at her. "For some of the people around here, that's an everyday occurrence. They don't know what *they* are doing, let alone what anyone else is up to, and *every* day is a surprise. But I see your point. Some things we're better off not knowing until they happen."

On the day of the auditions, would-be talent showed up in droves. The committee had thought to limit the acts but, as LeeAnne said, "We can't possibly leave anyone out, someone's feelings might get hurt." So, for better or worse, we were going to be subjected to the full extent of geriatric talent that Golden Harvest had to offer. I could hardly wait. Yeah, right!

Since I wasn't performing, I had been coerced into the role of publicity chairperson. Two weeks before the big debut, Maggie, LeeAnne and I sat around my table, elbow deep in poster board and markers. LeeAnne sketched on a piece of card stock we had bought for mock-ups of our finished posters.

"The participants got together and decided the program should be open to the public," she said.

"Next thing you know, they'll want to buy a bus and take the show on the road," I huffed as I took notes on what information to put on the posters. I scribbled down the dates with a black marker—June 27th, 28th, and 29th. This was turning into a major production—and getting in the way of solving our crime.

LeeAnne laughed. "I don't think we're ready for a road show yet, but I must admit, I'm having a lot of fun, and Janine is floating on the proverbial cloud nine."

"Humph." I growled, "Maybe she'll fall off that cloud and crack her skull. Have you forgotten," I asked her, "that our main objective here is to keep an eye on Annie? And, while I'm asking questions, why are we being subjected to three days of this nonsense?"

Maggie patted my arm. "It's not nonsense, Helen, it's a fun diversion for all of us. On Friday the program will be a dress rehearsal in front of the residents. The Saturday evening and Sunday matinee performances will be open to the public."

"Right," agreed LeeAnne. "For those performances we will have a donation jar and all the proceeds will go to the local Outreach and food bank. Everyone thought it was a great idea to give something back to the community."

I dropped my gaze and doodled aimlessly on my paper. It was a good idea. Several Golden Harvest residents volunteered at Outreach, and there was a tub in the office where recyclable items and non-perishable items could be placed. Outreach had filled a great need in our community, and I suddenly felt very selfish for my single-minded efforts.

"Maggie, you're right," I sighed, "I am like that mouse-chasing dog of yours. I sometimes get focused on one thing and miss the bigger picture."

My friends both smiled as if this was an intervention and they—or I—had finally made a breakthrough.

"And," said LeeAnne, "I haven't forgotten about Annie. I've engaged her in some idle chitchat about Rick Garrison, but she shrugs it off and changes the subject. I noticed one thing, though; she keeps her file cabinet locked and has the key on a chain around her neck. To get her reaction, I asked if we might be able to use one of the drawers for program information. She was adamant that the cabinet was stuffed to capacity and couldn't possibly hold any more. I thought that a bit odd."

Maggie shook her head. "Maybe you're picking up vibes from Helen and trying desperately to create intrigue where there is a perfectly logical explanation."

I should have taken offense to that comment, but I was too busy trying to figure out how to break into Annie's file cabinet.

Chapter 27

A Comedy of Errors

The next couple of weeks everyone was caught up in rehearsals for the big production. Ora Price complained that Bingo attendance was down because of "all the foolishness", but gloated that she had been the recipient of many more winning cards.

I wandered by Annie's office in the rec-room to steal glances at that file cabinet. I even attended a couple of scrapbooking sessions to see if there was any way to get it open. I wished I had a set of lock picks like another one of my novel heroines, a PI who uses any means available to solve crimes. But from what I read in her books, those things aren't easy to use anyway. I couldn't very well stand around sticking wires into Annie's file cabinet while the oldsters cut and pasted pictures of their families.

One day I managed to fall against the cabinet; I grabbed one of the drawer handles and pulled hard as I pretended to lose my balance. It was locked up tighter than a rusty hinge. Annie looked at me and shouted, "Helen, what are you doing?" Then, as an afterthought, she added, "Are you okay?"

I righted myself and leaned against the cabinet. "I'm fine.

It's a good thing this is heavy," I said, patting the metal file. "What's in here anyway, lead or gold bars?"

"No, no," she stammered, leading me to a chair on the far side of the room, "it's just old files and odds and ends of craft supplies." She sat me down and continued to fawn over me. "Are you sure you didn't get any bumps or bruises? Maybe you should go see the nurse."

I shoved her away and stood up. "I'm perfectly alright. But I think I'll take a rain check on the scrapbooking for today." I waved my hand at the few other people in the room who were suddenly all eying me. "You go help the others. I'll see myself back to my room."

I stomped down the hall more curious than ever about the contents of that cabinet. Those must be some important odds and ends for Annie to keep them under lock and key. I tried to talk to Maggie and LeeAnne about this development but they were so involved in the upcoming production they didn't have time to discuss what they called "my little problem". LeeAnne I could understand, she was helping to produce this farce; but what was Maggie up to?

"Oh Helen, don't ask," she giggled. "It's a surprise."

I couldn't believe my ears. "Do you mean you are actually going to do something in that talent show? No offense, but what? You can't carry a tune in a bucket, and I don't see you as a dancer or a juggler."

She fluttered her hands in the air. "Don't even try to guess. You'll never figure it out. Suffice it to say it's a little out of character for me, and I'm having a ball!"

LeeAnne wasn't any help, either. "Helen, I'm not going to give you any information about the performers. You'll just have to wait like everyone else."

I began to wonder if LeeAnne had loaned Maggie some of her scarves and feathered fans, but discarded that idea. My friend may be breaking into show business, but she was of neither the age nor the temperament to take up fan dancing. Surely that couldn't be it! But she had been doing some strange things lately—like taking up with Lumley. Maybe strutting around behind feathers was the next step in her late-life crisis.

I used to believe I could read Maggie like an open book, but lately that book's pages were written in some foreign language to which I was not privy. I told myself I was concerned for her welfare, but actually I was afraid Maggie was moving into a territory into which I didn't fit and would have no part. I considered my fall from Maggie's graces and suddenly realized how petty I was being. My friend was laughing and enjoying life again and I should be happy for her. Things might be different, but we would always be friends. I could only hope my old friend was not going to embarrass us both by gyrating around on stage with feathers and scarves.

Everyone was in high spirits on opening night for our dress rehearsal. The local print shop had volunteered to print programs since the community was going to benefit from the production. Our posters and flyers had been well received and price of admission had been extended to include canned and boxed goods as well as monetary donations. Several people from "outside" showed up on opening night, mostly family members of the participants. A special invitation had been issued to the mayor and the coordinator of the outreach center, who both were in attendance. Someone had thought to bring boxes for the donations and they were filling up fast. A huge pickle jar with a slot cut into the lid served for the cash and it, too, was already half full. A catering company donated one hundred-fifty folding chairs and, with our dining room chairs added, over two hundred could be seated in the large area.

Annie greeted guests warmly as they filed into the room. As I approached she jumped back, startled, and grabbed the donation jar. I frowned at the action, she composed herself, smiled, and said, "Isn't this exciting?"

I peered around her into the room at the rows of seats. "You folks are undoubtedly expecting quite a crowd."

She beamed. "You can't imagine. The calls haven't stopped since the flyers went up. Even the newspaper called! They're sending a reporter to cover the show!"

Someone wanting to make a donation captured her attention. I took a program, wandered into the dining room-turned-auditorium, and wondered if I ought to keep an eye on Annie and that pickle jar. I plopped down in the front row and checked out the stage. Rollaway curtains separated the chairs from the stage area. A glance at the program confirmed the raised platform was also furnished compliments of Conroy's Catering. The rolling curtains vaguely resembled something from an old hospital ward, but, since there was no way to hang a curtain, they served the purpose.

At precisely 7 p.m. Jamie Cunningham whisked his way through the curtains carrying a portable microphone to welcome us to the "First Annual Golden Harvest Talent Show". A roar of applause and whistles sounded up behind me. Imagine my amazement when I turned and saw the place was packed. Now I really hoped Maggie wasn't going to make with the fans! Jamie introduced the organizers of the program. LeeAnne and Janine stood, Annie waved, keeping her hand on the pickle jar.

LeeAnne came to the front, took the mike from Jamie and thanked everyone for their support. "Now, without further adieu," she announced, "we will begin our show, most appropriately, with Shakespeare's soliloquy, "All The World's A Stage", by our own Janine Hopgood." She gestured toward the curtains, at which time, Ora Price and Marvin Oglevie pulled them back to reveal Janine in a flowing white toga-like garment. Although I was in the front row, I could hear the nods and sighs behind me as Janine recited through the ages of man. Now that we at Golden Harvest, as my grandson, Christopher, had pointed out to me recently, "were getting close to our expiration date", the recitation hit almost too close to home for some of us. All in all, it wasn't a bad performance—for Janine! And at least it wasn't the Snow Queen soliloquy!

As the curtain closed on the first act, someone wandered across the stage and everyone sniggered. The woman—I assumed it was a woman, anyway—wore a platinum blonde wig, a red, white and blue sequined bustier, red Speedos, support hose and nurses shoes, and carried a sign that read, "Wonder Woman, the Senior Years". When she reached the far side she turned the sign around and wandered slowly back across the stage with a confused look on her face. This sign read, "I wonder where I put my glasses?" Everyone laughed.

185

The curtains opened for the next act and I scanned my program. There it was in bold letters—**A Special Appearance by Wonder Woman.** No indication of who was playing the part. I shrugged as the act on stage caught my attention. June LaVelle was singing a rousing rendition of "At *The Bar, At the Bar, where I smoked my first cigar*". She was dressed in a blonde wig and red taffeta strapless gown under which she wore a tattered T-shirt. She clomped around the stage in combat boots, chewing on the cigar and occasionally flicking ashes on the floor. At the end of her song, she pursed her lips, threw the audience a big kiss; then she winked at Marvin, who almost ran over Ora with his half of the curtain as he pushed it closed. The applause and whistles hadn't died down yet when Wonder Woman stumbled back across the stage. This time her sign read, "I wonder if I took my meds?" She staggered off scratching her head.

After the third act, Wonder Woman's sign read, "I wonder what I came in here for?" And by the fourth act, the place was buzzing in anticipation of her next appearance.

The acts themselves weren't as bad as I had feared. The juggler didn't drop too many balls, the chorus line of old women and flabby old men in drag received lots of laughs. The singing ranged from the mediocre serious to LeeAnne's rousing, "You Can't Get a Man With A Gun". Even Jamie Cunningham got in on the act and, after his strong tenor voice sang "Danny Boy", there was not a dry eye in the house—including mine. I hated that. How can someone who sings like that be suspect of anything?

I could have done without Elsie Barstow and her dramatization of "The Highwayman", though. I was all too happy when Elsie and her Highwayman went riding, riding off into oblivion. She received polite applause for her efforts, and some actually seemed to enjoy it.

After Elsie and the Wonder Woman segment—this time "I wonder if it's almost over?"—the Jeepers Creepers Peepers closed the show. Wally—I'd never get used to calling him Bernie—had called me to ask what kind of music I liked. I told him smooth jazz was nice. I must admit, I was flattered that he had asked, and eagerly anticipated his performance—in a nice, friendly way, of course.

When Ora and Marvin drew the curtain back, Bernie stood there, center stage, confidant and smiling, to introduce his group. He motioned, pointing his tenor saxophone in her direction, "To my left, the lovely Rachel Miller, and her equally lovely piano stylings. And," gesturing behind him to the right, "Otto Flien on snares. We have worked up a little number," his smile this time directed squarely at me, "in honor of one of the residents who claims she likes smooth jazz. We call it "Sax at 2 a.m." He winked to the audience in general, received a chuckle from them, while I felt a blush emanate from my toes and end at the roots of my white hair follicles.

It must have been my imagination, but Wally/Bernie seemed to grow about six inches when he played that saxophone. The man was good while still allowing his fellow performers to share the spotlight. When the curtain closed on his performance, the audience exploded with a standing ovation.

Wonder Woman wandered back on stage carrying high a sign that read, "I wonder if I can hear one more song before bedtime?" The audience applauded and whistled even louder, chanting "Encore! Encore!"

187

The curtain opened one last time and the trio began some slow impromptu melodic notes until Otto slammed his snares and hollered, "Wait just a darn minute! Let's put some life in this party!" Rachel nodded, ran her fingers deftly over the keyboard and they began a raucous version of "Tiger Rag" that got everyone on their feet clapping and dancing in the aisles.

As the song wound down, LeeAnne came back on stage. "Thank you all for coming. We hope you enjoyed our little show."

The audience answered with rousing applause.

Janine joined her. "Don't forget, we have two more performances. All monetary and food donations go to the local outreach center. Tell all your friends!"

LeeAnne nodded and said, "Our special thanks to all the participants."

More applause.

"Especially Wonder Woman-The Senior Years!" She gestured stage right, and Wonder Woman walked back on stage with another sign, "I wonder if this is just another dream?" and grinned at me. I gasped. I'd know those sparkling teeth anywhere – Maggie Taylor!

She took a bow, and everyone cheered, no one louder than me!

As we left the auditorium I noticed Annie, the full pickle jar and all the donations were gone.

Chapter 28

How Do You Get to Carnegie Hall? Practice!

A nnie showed up Saturday with an empty pickle jar. The crowd packed our auditorium even tighter than for the Friday performance, and was met with as much enthusiasm. Now that I knew Wonder Woman's identity, I was impressed and proud of the changes in Maggie. I was also secretly relieved she had not opted to do a fan dance. I guess Lumley had to be given some credit for drawing out this playful side of my dear friend. That would make it all the worse if it turned out he was involved in the shenanigans going on at this place. I couldn't shake the feeling there was something about him that was not quite right. I just didn't know yet what it was. All that glass and chrome boardroom furniture in his apartment—and the world map with the pushpins in it—what was that all about? Maggie would hear none of it, and LeeAnne sided with her, so I had no one with whom to discuss my concerns.

After the Sunday matinee, the mayor took the stage and invited the whole troupe to do a performance at Loblolly's community center the following weekend. The town had a huge open-air amphitheater that could accommodate a larger audience.

189

The mayor promised to advertise the production countywide; after all, the food bank and outreach helped the whole county. Everyone thought that was a grand idea. It seemed they were all, like Janine, getting star-struck.

As we stood around the refreshment table toasting the participants, LeeAnne said, "Isn't it exciting how well-received our little show was?"

I held up my Styrofoam glass of watered-down punch. "Yes. And here I thought I was making a joke when I suggested y'all might buy a bus and take the show on the road. Guess the joke's on me."

"The community center isn't exactly taking the show on the road," LeeAnne smiled, "but it's a start." She raised her glass to mine and toasted in a loud voice, "Today the community center, tomorrow Carnegie Hall."

Several others raised their glasses and echoed, "Hear! Hear!"

Jamie Cunningham walked up to the table to congratulate the organizers. "LeeAnne, you and Janine did a marvelous job of putting this together. We collected seven large boxes of dry and canned goods for the food bank, plus all the money the show took in."

LeeAnne asked, "Do you have any idea about how much we raised?"

"Yes," he answered, "I helped count it after each performance. The shows raised nearly a thousand dollars. I gave Annie a bank bag to keep it in and offered to put the cash in the office safe until we can get a truck to haul everything over to outreach, but she said she would lock it up in her own office."

Maggie raised an eyebrow in my direction, and LeeAnne

looked around. "Where is Annie?" she asked. "I agree the money should be put in the safe. I'll go see if I can find her."

Jamie spoke up. "She already left. She said she had company coming to her house this evening, and said to tell you she would see you tomorrow." He wandered through the crowd, patting the new stars on the back and complimenting them on the success of the show.

My friends and I put our heads together to confer about this development. Maggie was the first to speak. "The nerve of that woman to latch onto money ear-marked for charity. How dare she?"

LeeAnne touched Maggie's arm and spoke in a reassuring voice, "Now, Maggie, calm down. We don't know that she's done anything wrong. She probably locked the money bag in her file cabinet; we know she keeps that thing secure."

"LeeAnne is right, Mags," I added. "She wouldn't dare steal the proceeds from the show. Especially since Jamie Cunningham helped count it."

Maggie huffed, "Look who's becoming the voice of reason. Are we doing role-reversal now?" she smiled at me.

"Yeah," I said. "I'm you, and you are Wonder Woman. Nice bustier, by the way. How did you ever fill the cups of that thing out?"

She slapped my arm playfully, leaned closer and whispered, "LeeAnne has falsies in all sizes!"

My mouth dropped open and my eyes bulged as I looked from Maggie's false cleavage to LeeAnne. She grinned and shrugged.

I regained my voice, and said, "I don't know why or how you managed to keep this escapade from me. I could have helped you with your signs or something."

She gave me a hug, the sequins on her bustier scraped across my arm. "Elsworth helped. I wanted to surprise you."

I attempted to locate a safe way to hug her in return. "You certainly did that! I didn't recognize you until you took your curtain call at the end of Friday night's show. You can hide a lot from me, but there's no mistaking your pearly whites or that smile. I just can't believe it took me so long to figure it out. Wonder Woman, indeed!" I laughed and hugged her again.

Just then Elsworth strode up beside Maggie, draped his arm casually across her shoulder, bent down and kissed her ear. "How's my Wonder Woman?" He nodded and smiled at me. "Helen." Then he raised his punch cup to LeeAnne. "Congratulations on a wonderful show. Sounds like it may have a longer run than some Broadway productions."

LeeAnne nodded. "Thanks. You may be right; the show seems to have taken on a life of its own." She winked at Maggie and smiled at Lumley. "Maggie and I thought we might add some more acts to our next performance. You and Helen must have some hidden talents we could incorporate into our production."

Lumley held up his hands in mock defense. "I can't speak for Helen, but I'm best suited to sit in the audience. I can't sing, but my whistles and applause can be heard far and wide. And they're much more appealing than anything I could do onstage."

"I have to agree with Elsworth," I said. "I can clap my hands almost in rhythm. And I can be counted on to laugh at most of the appropriate times."

I felt someone touch my elbow. "I hope your reaction to me was on the applause side." I turned to find Wally/Bernie's deep blue eyes smiling up at me.

"Of course. The jazz ensemble was magnificent. I never knew you were so talented. Your act was definitely high on my applause-o-meter."

Elsworth nudged him with his elbow. "That Sax at 2 a.m. line was pretty funny, though. Was it meant for anyone in particular?"

Bernie blushed, looked at me and I glanced at a point over his head on the far side of the room. "No, no," he said, "Simply an ice-breaker. Something to lighten everyone's mood—and help our ensemble get over our stage-fright."

Lumley patted his back. "Well, good job." He turned to Maggie. "How about some frozen yogurt at the ice cream shop?"

Her blue eyes sparkled as she looked up into his steel-gray ones. "That sounds good. Let me go slip into something a bit less provocative." As she slipped away, Elsworth asked if any of us would like to ride along, but we all declined. Privacy was difficult enough to come by around here, without a bunch of us tagging along when a couple wanted to go for ice cream.

After they left, Bernie asked if I'd care to take a stroll around the garden.

"I'm not much in the mood for strolling anyplace," I said.

"Oh, that's fine. I should probably go to my apartment. It's just such a nice night…"

"You're right," I added quickly, "it is a nice evening. We could sit outside and get some fresh air, and you could tell me more about this talent you've kept so well hidden."

"That's great. I'd like that. Not talking about me—but visiting would be nice."

193

He took my cup. "Let me go freshen our punch and I'll meet you outside."

LeeAnne grabbed hold of my arm as he walked away. "Looks as though the success of his performance has bolstered Bernie's courage. You be nice to him, Helen."

I clutched my chest and gave her my best shocked expression. "Me? I'm always nice. Nice is my middle name!"

"Yeah, okay," she said, "let's go with that, shall we?'She patted my arm. "You and Mr. Peepers have a nice visit. I'm going to go crash in my apartment. I'm bushed. I'll see you all tomorrow."

I wandered out to the garden and sat down. Why did I agree to this rendezvous? I had already convinced myself Wally/Bernie and I were ill suited. *You ninny, this is not a life-long commitment you're making; it's a casual visit with a friend in the garden, nothing more.*

And so it was settled—at least in my mind. I wasn't sure what Bernie's take would be on our get-together.

I watched as he pushed his back against the door to open it, his hands full with our punch cups. He handed me one and sat down tentatively beside me on the stone bench.

"Thanks, Wally—I mean Bernie," I said, taking a sip of the punch. "It will take some getting used to for me to remember your real name, I'm so used to thinking of you as Wally." I began babbling about names and the weather and lord knows what else and, for some reason, couldn't stop myself. Nervous chatter. What was I nervous about? It was only Wally—Bernie, I reminded myself for the umpteenth time. There was nothing about him that should invoke a case of nerves. I finally ran out of idle topics and

194

apologized. "I usually don't talk this much. I don't know what got into me."

"Perhaps it's the punch." He raised his cup to his mouth and took a sip. "Besides, I like to listen to your voice. It's very," he thought a moment, "lyrical."

No one had ever said my voice was lyrical. Piercing, maybe. Antagonistic, most definitely. But lyrical? Never. I sniffed my drink cautiously. It smelled okay. I ran my fingers around the top of the cup and asked, "You didn't lace this with anything, did you?"

His laugh put me at ease. "No, I assure you, I didn't put anything into your punch. I hope I don't appear to be as untrustworthy as that."

I took another sip of punch and assured him he did not. But, I thought, that trust did not spill over to the Cunningham's or Lumley. And I definitely had a gnawing concern about Annie and the money in that pickle jar.

Chapter 29

All Shook up

Bernie smiled and I felt my cheeks grow warm. I hoped I wasn't as visibly shaken as I felt inside. I *couldn't* be falling for him; the idea was too ludicrous! Was it that tenor saxophone or the way his blue eyes sparkled when he smiled that caused my reaction? Whatever the reason, he had stirred up sensations that had lain dormant for years. In fact, they may have been hibernating all my life. I couldn't recall a time I had searched out the company of a man. And now, when the feelings had been awakened, here sat 5'7", balding, Bernie Cox with his mellow sax and smiling eyes. If I ever hugged him I'd probably crush his ribs! I gulped down another swallow of the punch. I secretly hoped it *was* laced with something; I needed the courage. Determined to gain control of the situation and the conversation, I asked, "So, how long have you been playing the saxophone?" That seemed like safe enough territory.

"Oh, oh. I feel an interview coming," he teased.

I snapped my fingers. "As a matter of fact, that's not a bad idea. I could use some material for the newsletter." I jumped up, glad for the distraction. "I'll go get my note pad and be right back." I walked across to my door and turned to face him, "Or you could come inside and we could visit in my apartment." I mentally kicked myself. Why had I suggested that? I'd be right up there with Marvin Oglevie on the gossip list when people found out!

Perhaps he sensed my discomfort—or perhaps my scrunched-up face, tight-shut eyes and the doubled-up fist in my mouth were indicators. Whatever the reason, Bernie declined, and said he would rather sit outside where we could enjoy the fresh air and the lovely evening. I breathed a sigh of relief, ran inside, grabbed my legal pad, returned to the garden and began the interview. After a few preliminary questions—Where did he grow up? Central Alabama. His age? Seventy-one. His first saxophone had been handed down to him from some relative. He and a couple of his high school buddies, one who had a guitar and the other who beat out rhythm on an old wash basin, used to get together and make noise.

I grimaced. "Sounds lovely."

He laughed. "We were awful at first, but we improved enough that we got asked to play at some of the local dances." He grinned, "But two guys with a comb, some waxed paper and kazoo would have been called a dance band in my neck of the woods."

He said after high school he had played up and down the East coast, sitting in with local jazz bands on nights and weekends while holding down a paying job as a salesman. He spoke fondly of individuals and groups with whom he had played. Some he swore, were famous—at least to other jazz musicians. I had never heard of any of them; names like Blind Willy and Salty Pepper, Duke and the Dangles, Mama Jo Roberts, Dog-ear Barkley and Chow Down Duncan.

I scanned his face to see if he was telling the truth. "You're joking about some of those folks—like Dog-Ear and Chow Down—aren't you? They sound like cartoon characters."

He held up his hand in the scout salute. "Scout's honor. Dog-Ear Barkley had a cauliflower ear that looked as though some mutt had chewed on it. In fact, his whole appearance was that of a stray dog; but he was gentle as a kitten and played a mean bass. And Chow Down Duncan had two loves, playing piano and eating. He courted both lovers until he dropped dead on a stage up in Freeport." He smiled, a far-away look in his eyes. "He weighed five-sixty and had to be buried in a piano case. Very fitting end, actually." He nodded his head and sighed. "He would have approved."

The statement seemed to demand a moment of silence for Chow Down, forever at rest in his piano case coffin. Besides, no zippy one-liners came to mind. I sat quietly tapping my pen against the note pad for what I hoped was an appropriate length of bereavement time before asking my next question. "So, Bernie, did you have a stage name?"

He grinned at me and raised an eyebrow. "Now you're getting personal!"

I found it easy to talk to him; conversation was comfortable in a way I hadn't expected it to be. "Sounds like all the names are personal—and some of them not too complimentary at that."

"It may sound that way to an outsider, but musicians are a close-knit bunch; we have great respect for one another. The names are, in some strange way, an extension of that respect." He half-smiled, half-frowned, that tentative look of one seeking approval or validation. "Does that make sense, at all?"

I nodded, trying to recall a time when a gentleman had sought validation or approval from me. It was nice to think that someone besides Maggie might actually care about my opinion. "Yes, I guess so," I said. "But you still haven't told me what the others called you."

He dropped his gaze as if embarrassed, and mumbled, "You've got to promise not to laugh if I tell you."

I crossed my heart. "I promise. After all, it can't be worse than Dog-Ear or Chow Down, can it?"

"I suppose not." He shrugged, again with the grin. "People called me Tall Boy." He rushed on without giving me a chance to make any comment. "I used to carry around one of those tall skinny glasses that looks as though it holds a lot more than it actually does. I'm not much of a drinker, but when you play in some of the joints I did, you have to maintain an appearance. People joked, "Here comes Bernie with his Tall Boy". Then some folks started commenting that I actually looked taller when I was playing, and the name stuck. You know," he leaned closer and touched my arm, "I really do feel like I gain a few inches when I get a tune or a tone just right. There's something almost magical about it."

I had seen some of that magic when he was on stage. Should I—could I—admit that to him? Did I want to admit to myself that Tall Boy Bernie Cox and his saxophone had somehow bewitched me the moment he started playing?

"Uh, yes," I stammered, "the saxophone does have a mesmerizing tone."

"I'm mesmerizing, huh?"

I quickly jumped to my next question.

Bernie held up his hands. "That's enough about me. I want to find out what makes Helen Patterson tick."

I was used to being the asker not the askee, and I found myself rambling on again. "There's nothing special about me, nothing interesting like with you and LeeAnne. Why, even Janine the Snow Queen saved Christmas back in seventh grade!" I smiled but suddenly realized how boring my whole life had been; drab in comparison to playing saxophone in a smoky bar with the likes of Dog-Ear, Chow Down and Mama Jo Roberts, or waving feathers and fans. "I lead a very dull life," I sighed.

Bernie pulled one of our business cards from his pocket. "What about the Tricycle Girls Investigation? That sounds exciting to me. What's that all about? I've never known a private detective before."

I scoffed, "It's not a real detective firm; we don't have licenses or even any clients, for that matter. We're only checking out a few things around here. It's mostly a mental exercise, like solving a logic puzzle."

"I'm sure it's much more than that." He nudged my arm. "Do you carry a gun?" He had a broad grin and a twinkle in his eye.

"No, but I swing a mean nine-iron!"

"Ouch!" he said. "I think I would rather be shot. It's quicker than getting beat to death with a golf club."

He leaned close and whispered like James Cagney in some B movie, "Word on the street is you're investigating the missing items from the residents' apartments. Have you turned up any clues or suspects?"

"As a matter of fact," I confided, "Elsworth Lumley is high on my list."

He leaned back, a puzzled look on his face. "Lumley? I admit he's different, but that's not a crime. Do you have any specific reasons to suspect him?"

I listed my reasons, valid or not. I began with his sudden move here just before all the strange things began happening and ended with the pushpins in his world map. "Besides," I concluded, "there's something about him that's just not right. I think he's hiding something."

Bernie folded his arms across his chest. "What do your partners think about your assessment?"

"Maggie and LeeAnne?" I threw my hands in the air. "Maggie, as everyone can see, is so taken with him, she won't even discuss the possibility; and LeeAnne is on her side. I'm afraid Maggie is going to get hurt, and I can't stop it."

Bernie put his hand gently on my shoulder. "Maggie is a big girl, she can take care of herself. But I see what you mean about Mr. Lumley. If you would like, I could keep an eye on him for you. Maybe I can catch him up. I read lots of mysteries, and always wanted to be Travis McGee or Mike Hammer."

I grabbed his arms, "Would you? That would be great! I can't keep track of everyone by myself. And something Lumley said makes me think Maggie might be in danger."

"Of course, Helen. Anything for you." He leaned forward, gave me a peck on the cheek and added, "Helen Patterson, you are an intriguing woman."

Flustered by that show of emotion, I stood up and began to absent-mindedly brush invisible lint off the front of my blouse. Intriguing, huh? No one had ever said that of me, either. My usual repertoire of snappy comebacks failed me once again. Part of me wanted to continue this flattering conversation, while the sensible, self-reliant part screamed, "Run as fast as your arthritic knees and artificial hip will allow!"

The moment of infatuation passed and Bernie also rose to his full 5' 7", stretched and yawned. "It's been a busy weekend. Guess I'll hit the sack. Thanks for the wonderful visit, Helen."

"Yes," I stammered. "I have things to do, too. I need to type up my notes on the show and get your interview done for next week's newsletter."

He smiled and winked as he walked toward the door. "Make me look good. See you later." He let himself back into the main building and I crossed the patio, opened my apartment door, glided in and sat down at my computer. See you later? Was that an invitation? I stared at the face in the mirror; it didn't look intriguing—amused, maybe. It was really nice of Bernie to take such an interest in the investigation, I thought. It would also be helpful to have someone keep an eye on Lumley for me. I ran the conversation over in my mind. Come to think of it, he had sure been interested in particulars of the case. And what was that about whether I had a gun? Was he trying to discover if I was a threat to him?

I didn't want Bernie to be a suspect; after all, he had said I was intriguing! I groaned, and reluctantly added him to my list.

Chapter 30

Little Cottage in the Wood

With Bernie keeping an eye on Lumley, I could concentrate on other matters, and that's how I found myself the next day with LeeAnne in the grove of trees behind the Over-the-Hillton.

"Maybe we should start working out like Ora and the girls," LeeAnne wheezed as we worked our way down the path and into the grove of loblolly pines behind Golden Harvest. She clutched her chest. "My lungs are on fire."

"It's the heat and humidity," I choked back at her as I bent forward and placed my hands somewhere close to my knees. Perhaps the action would work like a bellows and pump some air into my own fiery airways. "Given a choice between being thrown into an erupting volcano and stretching spandex over my frame to ride a stationary bicycle, I'd gladly jump into the boiling lava. But that's just me."

"Exercise isn't that bad, it just takes getting used to," she said. "And, of course, the right outfit helps!"

"Hah! You've never seen me in spandex! Come on, we're almost there."

We were on our way to George's cottage that sat about a quarter mile behind the apartments, on a piece of wooded land he retained in the sale to the retirement home developers. It was built in typical cabin form and looked like an overgrown project from some giant child's set of those fit-together logs. I had been inside on several occasions; it was totally utilitarian: one bedroom, a study, and one bath. The small kitchen and living room was all one large, open area with a fireplace, constructed of local granite, on the back wall. The ceilings were beamed with raw timbers. All in all, the place had a very cozy, but masculine, feel. The arrangement had worked out well, and George was content here, conveniently located close to Golden Harvest; that is until this whole mismanagement idea, instigated by the Cunninghams, came up.

LeeAnne held her chest and continued to wheeze. "I suppose you're right about the heat. It really is stifling today. We should have waited until evening when it cools off."

"But in the evening, Frankie and Jamie are here. We need to check out the place without getting caught." I hoped that would be the case, anyway.

I didn't know what we were looking for or what I expected to find, but our investigation had stalled. I was antsy; I had to do something, even if it involved a little unwarranted snooping. Thus the trip to check out George's place, even though Jamie "Bones" and his cat-wife now called it home. Maggie was off playing footsie, I hoped not literally, with Lumley. That idea distracted me momentarily and I shook my head to clear the unwanted picture from my brain. I had conned—convinced—LeeAnne to join me on this excursion with the added incentive that a walk and fresh air would clear our heads. Unfortunately, the closer we stepped toward the cabin, the more muddied my thought processes became.

"What are we looking for? I hope you're not planning to break in. You're not hiding a set of lock picks, are you? I will not be a party to B & E."

Having her read those mystery novels was paying off; our new friend was adept at picking up the PI jargon. And today she was even better at whining!

"Just relax. You're going to worry yourself into a coronary! We're only making a friendly call. Will it be my fault if there's no one home when we get there?"

Perspiration beaded in the furrows on LeeAnne's forehead. "It might be, since you knew before we headed out on this tropical jaunt that there was no one home."

I flicked my hand in the air. "Details, details."

The cabin came into view and I trudged up the steps to the back porch, which faced Golden Harvest. "I'm not going to break in, but if the door happens to be unlocked, we won't be breaking into anything."

"The police might consider that fuzzy logic. I think the entering part is the worse of the two felonies," she said as she followed me up the steps.

I cocked my head as if in thought. "Do you think it's a felony or a misdemeanor?" I knocked twice then twisted the knob. "Darn! It's locked." I tried to peek through the window, but the drapes were drawn tight.

I descended the steps and LeeAnne sighed, "Good! Let's get out of here."

I edged toward the front of the house. "Might as well try the front door while we're here. I always have an open invitation to George's house."

She followed close on my heels; any closer and she'd have been riding piggyback. "You forget," she growled, "George doesn't reside here anymore."

I turned and she ploughed into me. I placed my hands on my hips and glared down into her green eyes. "Don't say that! Don't even think that! This *is* George's home. He *does* reside here—or will, again, as soon as we get to the bottom of whatever it is that's going on around here!"

She reached out and patted my arms. "Okay, okay. Calm down, Helen. I'm sorry. I phrased that wrong. I just wanted to remind you, at this particular time, this is not George's place of abode. I'm afraid the police might consider you had overstepped the bounds of friendship by entering a house which, although the legal property of a friend, was not, at the time in question, inhabited by said friend."

I gawked at her, my mouth open, chin hanging. "Jeez, were you an attorney in a former life?"

She folded her arms across her chest. "I watch a lot of court TV. Sounded pretty impressive, didn't I?"

"I guess." I grabbed her arm. "Let's check out that door."

She shook her head in resignation and followed me. The front door was also locked, as were all the windows.

"Can we go now, please? I do not want to get caught peeking in windows and have to explain my presence here."

The woman's whining was getting on my nerves. I turned and headed down the path that would lead us back through the piney woods to the Golden Harvest. "Might as well, we can't get inside."

As we walked away, I heard the distinct sound of tires crunching on gravel. LeeAnne and I both gasped and snuck deeper into the grove of trees as fast as we could toddle. We had missed getting caught by the dastardly duo by only a few steps. We were both out of breath, and our heart rates were elevated, when we hit the safety of the building, dashed in and collapsed into the nearest chairs in the entryway. We looked wide-eyed at each other and tried to laugh, but we were too winded.

"Close call," I finally managed.

LeeAnne nodded, her hand still on her chest. "Too close."

Chapter 31

Six Sneaky Suspects

When we finally were able to breathe normally—or at least were able to quit gasping like a couple of trout out of water, LeeAnne raised herself from the chair. "I think I'll remove myself to the relative solitude of my apartment." She listed to one side, grabbed the wall for support and said, "If you call me later about another harebrained scheme, I'm not answering my phone. In fact, I'm going to turn the ringer off and take a nap!" She straightened her back and shoulders and stepped decisively down the hall away from me.

"You know you had fun," I said to her retreating figure.

She turned, cocked an eyebrow and shook her head in a way that said, "What-am-I-going-to-do-with-you?"

I smiled and waved. "See you at dinner."

She raised her hand in the air and nodded without looking back again.

I dragged myself to my feet. I wasn't used to this much exertion. I knew that the next day LeeAnne and I were both going to feel the effects of our afternoon "walk". Maybe we *should* get into an exercise program, or at least do some power stretches, before our next jaunt. I had a feeling, though, that it would take some creative wheedling to convince LeeAnne to participate in another afternoon stroll with me. I limped back toward my room; my knees ached, and I had rubbed a blister on my pinky toe. It was going to take more than power stretching to get this old carcass in shape!

Bernie caught up with me as I tottered along, not a difficult thing to do in my gimpy state. "What happened, Helen? Did you twist your ankle?"

I took another step, stopped and grimaced. "Might as well have. But it's nothing that interesting. I have a blister on my toe. I'm on my way to put a bandage on it."

"Ouch! I won't keep you, then. Just thought you might want an update on your Mr. Lumley."

"He's *not* my Mr. Lumley, he's Maggie's Mr. Lumley," I said. "But hobble along with me and fill me in."

He had to walk slowly to match my labored pace. "There's not a lot to tell; he goes to town quite often, nothing unusual about that. The only person he spends any amount of time with is your friend Maggie. I've tried to engage him in conversation, but he's a man of few words."

"Yes, I found that out when I interviewed him for the paper. He was mysterious, reluctant to open up, and tried to cover it up by being charming."

"I have to agree with you that he's a mysterious character," he said, taking my elbow to steady me as I limped along. "But maybe that's just a persona he puts on."

We had made it to my door. "You mean you think it's all an act? He wants us to believe he's "Mr. Intrigue"?"

Bernie shrugged and held the door for me. "People have done stranger things to try to impress people. Why, I once knew a guy who took the name of a TV personality because someone told him he sort of resembled the star."

I turned to ask whom. He grinned from ear to ear and those dark blue eyes, magnified by his horn-rimmed glasses, sparkled like bubbles in champagne. I swatted his arm. "You were talking about yourself. Did you become Wally Cox to "get chicks", as my grandson would say?"

"No, no. I'm afraid impressing chicks is way out of my league." He stood there still holding my door open. I finally asked if he would care to come in.

"May I have a rain check? I have a date with a mystery novel and you have a toe to doctor."

"Sure," I stammered as he let go of the door and touched my shoulder.

His hand floated down my arm and he gave my elbow a light squeeze that sent a tingle up my arm and down my spine. "I'll hold you to it, then." He backed into the hallway. "By the way, when is that flattering article about me going to hit the presses?" Again those twinkling eyes flustered me.

I cleared my throat and attempted to retrieve some of my abrasive attitude. "The paper will be out on Friday, as usual. I made you look so good the ladies around here will flock to you in droves."

"Oh, no. I don't want *all* the ladies flocking. I couldn't handle that."

I gave him my best nonchalant smile. "Try it, you might like it."

"I don't think so. Is that some more of your grandson's "chick" advice?"

I laughed. "No, that one probably came from his grandfather.

My ex-husband was a great believer in trying out new things."

"Do I detect a slight edge in your voice? How about we pursue this subject at a later date?" He started down the hall and waved. "Can't wait to read how you portrayed me in the paper; and I'll cash in that rain check soon. Now go doctor your toe before you get an infection."

I closed the door and rubbed my arm where Bernie had caressed it. I couldn't think of a better word. First a peck on the cheek, then an arm caress. What next? Footsies? Nibbling on an ear? Full-on mouth kissing? What would I do if he tried any of those things? The very thought made me hyperventilate which, in turn, brought me back to reality. *Get a grip; you're a seventy-year-old woman, you can deal with this.* Truth was, I liked Bernie, and I liked the way I felt when he was around—well, except for the uncomfortable fact that I made nearly two of him. No way could my mind wrap itself around that. What would people think?

Then it dawned on me—I'd never before worried about how people perceived me. I hobbled to the medicine cabinet for my peroxide and bandages and sat down at the table. I rubbed my arm again; I swear it was warm from Bernie's electric touch. *But he's only five-foot-seven.*

I'd seen those TV shows that showcased women who fell for midgets or scrawny little men, and wondered at the attraction. *But Bernie isn't a midget or scrawny,* I reminded myself; *he's compact. And he can really play that saxophone. But that's not much of a foundation on which to build a relationship—and he's only 5' 7".* We'd resemble some kinky circus duo when we walked down the street. I put my elbows on the table and dropped my head into my hands. I was a mess and, I suddenly realized, I was a height bigot!

I alternated between feelings of stupidity and guilt; and after I thoroughly beat myself up mentally, I kicked off my shoe and doctored my toe. I considered leaving it unbandaged as a reminder of my now guilt-ridden dilemma, but physical discomfort wouldn't solve anything, and I was not an advocate of pain. I opted for denial, always a better choice. I could do denial!

I grabbed my legal pad and gel pen to make a list of our suspects in the pending case.

First on the list were the Cunninghams, for all the obvious reasons; mainly because I was angry that they marched in here and took George's job. All the other shenanigans started after their arrival.

Next was Elsworth Lumley because he was way too mysterious. And, even if he had stolen nothing else, he took my best friend's heart, and I didn't want it to get broken.

Third were Annie James and/or Rick Garrison. I thought about giving them the number two place on my list, but left Lumley there for strictly personal reasons. Annie and Rick had made all those suspicious trips to the pawnshop. And I still wanted to know what she kept in that locked file cabinet. She and Rick had also started working here recently, and at about the same time. And Annie had been acting really strange lately. Everywhere I went, I could feel her eyes on me. What did we know about their backgrounds? I could have asked George if he was still around, but I was sure Frankie the Cat wouldn't give me any information.

Next were Kate McGinnis and possibly her husband, Stanley, only because she had shown such an interest in organizing the antique jewelry club—Genealogy by Jewelry, or some such rot. Not an unusual endeavor for a clubwoman like Kate, but suspicious because it coincided with the disappearances.

Lennie the handyman was way down on my list, his only obvious connection being he had a master key to all the apartments. Motive? Perhaps he thought he could offer precious gems to the aliens when they beamed him up to their ship for their experimental purposes.

I put Bernie at the very bottom. He had asked some questions about the case, but was, in my mind at least, an even less likely suspect than Lennie the space cadet.

I checked my updated list to see if I had forgotten anyone, or if the real perpetrator's name would suddenly be underlined in red or highlighted in fluorescent orange. No such luck. My phone jarred me into real time. It was Maggie.

"Helen, have you heard? Sandy Germain's Swiss timepiece is missing!"

My ears perked up. "What was left in its place?"

"A wedge of Swiss cheese."

Naturally.

Chapter 32

Eenie, Meenie, Minie or Maggie

LeeAnne and I proceeded with difficulty to the dinner table that evening. Maggie was already there; the woman was always so disgustingly prompt.

"What's with you two? You dragged in like a couple of old ladies."

"Ha, ha," we said in unison as we plopped down in our chairs.

"We tried doing a little exercise today," LeeAnne said.

Maggie's mouth dropped open. "You mean you actually went to the gym?"

"No," I said. "We aren't that desperate. We just took a walk and I got a blister."

"And I got sore knees and calves and ankles," LeeAnne added. "In fact, except for my ears, and maybe my eating hand, there's not much of me that doesn't hurt!"

Maggie laughed. "What did you do, try to run a marathon?

"Something like that," I said as I glared at LeeAnne to not say any more. I picked up my tea to take a sip. I had never noticed before how heavy those iced tea glasses were.

"So, fill us in on Sandy Germain. Who told you, and when did it happen?" I glanced around the dining room. I was sure similar conversations were taking place at every table.

Maggie leaned forward. "When El and I returned from town, Phyllis Pomeroy met us at the door. According to her, Sandy found the cheese when she went back to her apartment after playing Bingo. She walked in and wondered what the strange smell was. She was about to call Lennie about a sewer problem when she discovered the slice of Swiss. She immediately made the connection, looked for her clock, and realized it was missing. From what Phyllis said, the Swiss was pretty ripe. As you're probably aware, old cheese has a very distinctive smell." She reached into her purse, pulled out a zip locked bag with the offending cheese inside, and held it out toward me with two fingers. "Sandy gave this to me to add to our collection."

"Oh, goody," I said, as I tentatively took the bag from Maggie's outstretched fingers. "The smell won't leech through that bag, will it?" I asked. I flipped it around and examined it. "I wonder if Rick has used Swiss cheese in any recipes lately?"

"As a matter of fact, he made chicken Cordon Bleu last week," said Maggie.

We eyed one another and Rick gained a notch on our suspect list.

"Speaking of Rick," said LeeAnne, "I was in the library earlier and noticed one of those cooking magazines in the trash. I thought it had been knocked in there by mistake, but when I picked it up, it was all torn up."

"What does that have to do with Rick?" asked Maggie.

I jerked my head in her direction and gasped. "What do you mean it was torn up? Torn up how?"

215

"Well, it was addressed to him at Golden Harvest and it looked as though some kindergarten class had cut out things all through the book."

"Probably left over from one of Annie's craft classes," Maggie said.

"Right," I agreed. But I wasn't so sure. It brought back to mind that note someone had sent me. "Speaking of Annie, have either of you found out any more about her comings and goings?"

They both shook their heads, but Maggie added, "Phyllis did tell me Annie had called in sick today. Ora sat in for her at Bingo. Phyllis referred to Ora as The Blind Bat Bingo Brawler."

"That's pretty good alliteration. I'll have to remember that one," I said. I turned to LeeAnne. "Has Annie turned in the donation money?"

She shook her head. "Not yet. And she'll have an army of angry senior citizen performers after her if she doesn't."

"That's a scary thought," I said.

We finished our dinner without much more conversation. Maggie told us about her trip to town with Lumley. They had gone to the second-hand bookstore where he had unearthed some real finds, First Editions of some of his beloved spy stories. Maggie reached into her bag again. "I found something for you, Helen." She pulled out a cookbook, flipped it open to page sixteen, and laid it in front of me. "See," she said, pointing to the middle of the page, "a recipe for homemade fig bars."

I slammed the small book closed, almost catching her fingers. "Oh, you are *so* funny!" They both laughed.

"I hope you don't really expect me to have fresh baked fig bars for you the next time you visit."

"No, that would be way too much to ask. It was pretty funny though; and the look on your face was priceless!"

I rolled my eyes. "Yeah, you're getting to be a real comedienne. That Wonder Woman routine has gone to your head."

After dessert, LeeAnne and I were ready to crash and Maggie had planned an evening stroll with El. LeeAnne and I had "strolled" enough for one day. We left Maggie at her door.

"I worry about Maggie getting hurt," I said as we reached LeeAnne's apartment.

"You worry too much," she said as she unlocked her door. I think Elsworth is one of the good guys."

"I hope so. But it was so much easier in the days of Saturday morning serials, when the good guys all wore white hats."

She nodded. "Ain't it the truth! Good night. I'll see you tomorrow—if I can manage to roll myself out of bed."

I limped away laughing. "Ain't it the truth!"

I unlocked my door, entered the apartment and flipped on the light. I closed the door behind me and turned the deadbolt. That's when I noticed another #10 envelope on my floor. I began to hyperventilate again, not the good, arm caress kind. This was the fear kind, the kind that makes your head ache and your lungs hurt.

I bent down, picked it up, carried it gingerly in front of me as if it was a bomb that needed to be diffused, and dropped it on the table. I sat down, put my chin in my hands and stared at the poisonous thing. I had suspected I might get another threat when LeeAnne mentioned the cut up magazine. I just wasn't expecting it this soon—or maybe I was in denial again.

I don't know how long I sat there staring—it seemed like

hours, but was probably just minutes. I finally took a deep breath and opened it. Another single sheet of paper and another of our business cards fell out. This note simply said: EENIE, MEENIE, MINIE, OR MAGGIE? At the bottom, instead of a signature, was a crudely drawn skull and crossbones.

What did that mean? I circled it around in my mind for a while before settling on what, I thought, was the only possible explanation. I picked up my purse and my keys, grabbed the note and my notes on our suspects, and headed out the door. I had to warn Maggie and LeeAnne!

I saw Lumley walking down the hall toward me as I headed to Maggie's apartment. "Hello, Helen. Where are you going in such a hurry?"

I glared at him. "Is Maggie in? I've got to talk to her."

"Yes, we just came back from a walk around the grounds. It's a lovely evening." He touched my shoulder. "Helen, you're shaking. What on earth got you so upset?"

I grabbed the note from my purse and shook it in his face. "Do you know anything about this?"

He took it from me and read through it several times. His expression didn't change, but his eyes darkened and he clenched the letter so hard his knuckles turned white. "Is this a joke?"

"If it is, it's a sick joke, and you had better not be a part of it."

"Helen," he said, "I swear I'm not. I hate to frighten you, but this note sounds like a threat."

"That's what I thought; and I'm way past frightened; I'm halfway to hysterical."

He took my arm. "Can we go someplace and discuss this? My apartment is close."

"No!" I shouted, pulling away from his grasp. "Not your apartment. Not my apartment, either. Someplace open."

"Certainly. How about the great room?"

I nodded. "I guess that would be fine."

The great room was a large open area with couches, chairs and a huge fake fireplace. Not too many people hung around there. Fireplaces that burned but gave off no heat were not a big draw to tired old bodies that didn't generate much heat of their own. But it was open; if Lumley had it in his head to do me in, he probably couldn't accomplish it in the great room.

When we were seated, Elsworth again tried to convince me he was on our side. Despite Maggie's insistence, I wasn't sure enough to trust him.

He raised the paper he still held in his hand. "Is this the first letter like this you have received?"

I shook my head. I wanted to believe he was a good guy. I wanted someone, if not bigger than me, at least more courageous than me, to ride in wearing his white hat and fix this.

"The first one came two or three weeks ago, right after I printed our business cards. At that time this whole thing was nothing more than a mental exercise, something fun to do besides play Bingo. I didn't think it would cause any harm." I choked back a sob. "But it's not fun anymore." I hugged myself to keep from flying into a million or so pieces.

Lumley spoke very softly and patted my arm. "You're doing fine. Unfortunately, you have fallen into something more sinister than it appeared on the surface, and you seem to be making someone very nervous."

I nodded again. It was the only action I could force out of

219

myself right then.

He continued, "What did the other note say?"

I shuddered. "It said, Play the game at your own risk." I hugged myself tighter.

He stood up and paced in front of me. "Did you not consider that a threat? Why didn't you say anything to the authorities?" His voice raised a couple of decibels, and I shrunk deeper into my chair.

He leaned forward, his face close to mine. I must have had the terrified look reserved for small cornered animals, because he lowered his voice. "I'm sorry, Helen. I didn't mean to frighten you even more." He sat down in the chair to my right and sighed. "Take your time; tell me about the note."

"At first," I said, "I was frightened, but who could I tell? And what could I say? Then I got angry, and after that I decided it was another amateur detective playing his own version of the game. But this note seems to indicate that one of us is in danger."

"Isn't that what I tried to tell you when you printed up those fool cards?"

A tear escaped down my cheek; I brushed my hand across my face and swallowed hard. I would *not* let Lumley see me cry!

"Here," he said, handing me a monogrammed handkerchief, gray, of course. "We're working on this problem. I'm trying to keep Maggie safe, but I can't watch out for all of you. If I beg you, will you concede your investigation to me?"

I sniffled and looked into those gray eyes. "You don't look like the begging kind."

"And you don't look like you make many concessions."

He smiled, a real smile that reached those eyes and beyond.

"Alright," I sighed. "I'll back off if it will keep my friends from getting hurt. So, what *can* I do?"

"Maggie told me you have a list. Who's on it?"

I hesitated. What if he wasn't my white-hat guy? "You mean besides you?"

His laugh was soft and soothing. Surely no one who laughed like that could be a bad guy. "Yes," he said, "besides me."

I pulled the list out of my purse and handed it to him. He read through it carefully, nodding occasionally. Finally, he folded it and put it in his pocket. "I'm impressed. You've done a very good investigative job. Are you sure you've never done this before?" A smile played at the corners of his mouth.

I grabbed the arms of the chair to pull myself up. "You're making fun of me!"

He placed his hand over mine. "Only a little. Mostly I'm making a feeble attempt at a compliment. Some of your facts may be erroneous, but your research is impeccable. I know police officers who aren't this thorough." He patted my hand and I sat back down. I could see now what drew Maggie to him. He definitely had charisma.

He continued, "I believe we can cross off a few of your suspects."

I cocked my head and gave him a half smile of my own. "Besides you?"

Again I heard that hypnotic laugh.

I gazed at him expectantly. "Is Bernie one of those we can cross off?"

"Ah, Mr. Cox." He winked. "Yes, I'd say your Mr. Cox is definitely a non-suspect."

I let out an audible sigh. He stood, held out his hand, and I let him help me to my feet.

"Can we keep this conversation between the two of us?" he asked. "I promise, everything will be cleared up very soon."

I was afraid to ask too many questions, I might not like the answers; but I did have one more. "You mentioned "we" earlier. Is someone working with you?"

"For the record," he said, "I'm retired."

"What are you, some kind of spy?"

I caught an almost imperceptible raise of an eyebrow. "Helen Patterson, you read way too many mysteries," and he left me there wondering if Elsworth Lumley was his code name.

FIG BARS

1 cup shortening
1/2 cup granulated sugar
1/2 cup brown sugar
1 egg
1/4 cup milk
1 tsp. vanilla
3 cups sifted flour
1/2 tsp. salt
1/2 tsp. soda
Fig filling

Cream shortening and sugars. Add egg, milk, and vanilla. Beat well. Sift together dry ingredients. Stir into creamed mixture. Chill 1 hour.

On well-floured surface roll ¼ of dough into 8X12 rectangle. Cut crosswise in six 2-inch strips. Spread about 2 tablespoons Fig Filling down center of three strips. Moisten edges and top with remaining strips. Press lengthwise edges together with floured fork. Cut in 2-inch lengths. Do the same for rest of dough. Bake on ungreased cookie sheet at 375 degrees about 10 minutes. Makes 4 dozen.

Fig filling: Combine 2 cups finely chopped dried figs, 1/2 cup orange juice, and dash of salt. Cook stirring occasionally, till mixture is thick, about 5 minutes. Cool.

Chapter 33

If a Body Meets a Body

After dinner the next day, LeeAnne invited Maggie and me to join her in her apartment for one of our after-dinner get-togethers. We had become increasingly comfortable in one another's company and had formed a relaxed camaraderie. We were, after all, the Tricycle Girls. Maggie, however, had begged off, saying she and El were planning an evening stroll around the grounds again and she wanted to go freshen up.

Once we were settled in her apartment, LeeAnne handed me a glass of one of her juice drinks of dubious origin, and I held it up to the fading light.

"You know," I said, "you'd better be careful around here; there was a time you might have been burned at the stake as a witch for mixing up this kind of concoction."

She raised her glass to mine, her green eyes twinkled. "How do you know I'm not?"

"You got me there. Those green eyes might be a give-away."

I took a sip of my juice. "How about mixing up a potion to tell us who Lumley really is, Witchy Woman."

"Oh, Helen, I don't know why you don't trust him; Maggie is

so happy, and Elsworth seems smitten with her as well."

"Smitten!" I choked on my juice, an easy enough thing to do with all those semi-solids floating in it. "That sounds like a word from one of those sex-filled romance novels Maggie's been reading." I threw my head back and offered up a saccharine performance of some raven-haired beauty in the throes of despair, hand sweeping across my brow. "Margaret was *smitten* with Lumford's craggy good looks." I clutched my breast. "All the time knowing his hatred of her father would be her undoing."

LeeAnne applauded. "Bravo! Bravo! Grand performance. Are you sure you were never on the stage?"

I shook my head and accepted the praise. "No, but I've read enough romance novels to know the scenarios by heart."

LeeAnne turned to interview mode. "I don't understand, though. What's your problem with Elsworth? It seems to me you are jealous of his attention to Maggie."

I had to admit that was partly true, but added, "There's something not quite right about him. I just haven't figured out yet what he's hiding." I couldn't tell her about my meeting with Lumley, he'd sworn me to secrecy. That didn't prevent me from wanting to know who he really was and what he was up to.

LeeAnne sipped her juice, cocked her head in thought. "He doesn't act like he's hiding anything from Maggie. His eyes don't seem to conceal anything when he looks at her. My Charlie used to have that look. It was as though he was hoping for my approval." She was quiet for a few moments, lost in her memories, before she continued. "Charlie always said my smile gave him the strength to go on."

I remained silent and squirmed in my chair. No one ever said my smile kept them going, although sometimes I could get people to *go* if I used the right sneer. Not quite the same thing, I guess.

She set her glass down and patted her knees with her hands. "Anyway, that's how Elsworth looks at Maggie—as though hoping she approves of him."

"Maybe," I said. "I just don't want her to get hurt. She's so trusting."

"And you're not. What happened to make you so cautious?"

I gave her a sketchy summery of Harry and his buxom bimbo.

"Ah," she said. "Now it makes sense. But, trust me, it was Harry's loss. You're a terrific person."

She picked up her glass and raised it in a salute. "To the Tricycle Girls; and, if my witching powers are working, here's to leaks in the buxom bimbo's saline implants."

We raised our glasses to the Tricycle Girls and salt water, and I chewed the remainder of my juice in comfortable silence.

I left LeeAnne's shortly after that and headed to the library to exchange my book and read the evening paper. The light had faded to a dusky red outside but the lights burned bright in the library. It was usually quiet there this time of night. I wanted to be alone for a while but wasn't ready to return to the confinement of my apartment. By the time I left the library a sliver of moon shone in the clear night sky. I became a bit nostalgic and thought Maggie and Lumley had picked a lovely night for a walk.

My phone was jingling madly when I let myself into my apartment, and the blinking light on my answering machine echoed its insistent ring. I crossed to answer it without switching on a light. As I took the last step to pick it up, my toe caught on something. My eyes began to adjust to the darkness as I lifted the receiver.

"Hello."

"Helen, this is Elsworth. Is Maggie with you?"

"No, she left LeeAnne and me after dinner." Panic suddenly hit me as frightening possibilities ran through my mind. I yelled into the phone, "What do you mean is she with me? She is supposed to be with you!"

He answered slowly, calmly, "We were supposed to meet on the outside patio to go for a walk. I waited on our regular bench, but she never showed up."

I clicked on the desk lamp beside the phone. "Something must be wrong. She wouldn't stand you up. Did you try her apartment?"

"Of course. I tried calling, then I went to her door. She's not answering."

I turned to begin the pacing that helped me think, and caught sight of something that had no right or reason to be in my apartment. There in my sitting room, two heavy-booted feet stuck out from behind my loveseat. I heard a high-pitched, unearthly cackle, a scream and then everything went black.

I opened my eyes and a face rippled into semi-focus. My terrified mind vaguely remembered something. I screamed again and pulled away from the hands that held mine.

A familiar voice echoed in my addled brain. "Helen, it's me, Elsworth. Are you alright?"

I rolled to one side, managed to drag myself into a sitting position with his help. I touched the back of my throbbing head and felt a big lump. I groaned and leaned against the kitchen cabinet.

"What happened? Did someone hit me?"

Elsworth examined my scalp. "The skin isn't broken, that's a good sign." He walked to the tiny fridge, released some ice cubes into a kitchen towel, rolled it up and handed it to me. "Here, put this on your head. It's possible you were struck, or perhaps you hit your head when you fainted."

Fainted? Then the recollection of those boots hit me; I grabbed my chest. My breathing became erratic, my heart pounded in my chest like a crazed calypso musician beating steel drums. I attempted to stand up but the effort was too much for me. I looked up at Lumley, my eyes as wide as a puppy afraid of storms. "What about the boots behind my love... my couch?" I whispered.

He wrapped his large hands around my arm and helped me to my feet. The man was strong, I'd have to give him that.

"Ah, yes, the boots. There is a body attached to them." He looked in that direction and gave a schoolboy grin as though he'd just told a marvelous joke. I followed his gaze and nearly swooned again.

He caught my arm. "Easy there. Do you want to sit down?"

I turned my gaze away from the boots. "Yeah, that's a good idea."

He led me to a chair as far away from the booted body as the space would allow.

"Who is it? Is he dead?"

Lumley grinned again. "Well, it's your body, I figured you might know who it is." He raised his eyebrows. "And to answer your second question, yes, he is quite dead."

I managed to steal another peek across the room. The handle of a golf club jutted out from under the couch. "Are you sure?" I stammered. "How can you be sure? Did you call 9-1-1?"

"Well," he drawled, "the bullet hole in his forehead was a pretty good indicator. And, yes, I called the authorities."

"Bullet hole?" I shrieked and pointed a shaky finger in the direction of those boots. "There is a dead man behind my couch with a bullet hole in his head! And that's all you've got to say?"

"Yes, that's about it." He shrugged, arms outstretched. "Were you expecting something more?"

The irritating man was actually enjoying my hysteria! Suddenly I was on my feet and headed toward that golf club. Elsworth moved across the room as if jettisoned and grabbed my arm as I bent to pick it up. "This golf club doesn't belong here!" I said.

He grabbed me mid-stride. "Don't touch that!" He guided me back to my chair. "In fact, don't touch anything, you might destroy evidence. It's possible you were struck with that club. This is a crime scene. Forensics will have to determine what is important."

Crime scene? Forensics? The man had suddenly switched to secret agent or CSI mode and had claimed my apartment as his personal area of investigation. I wondered again who Elsworth Lumley really was.

My hands were shaking and tears came to my eyes. I was a wreck, and not used to dealing with a weepy version of me. Emotions were for other people; I was too strong to fall apart.

"Maggie," I stammered. "I've got to call Maggie."

Elsworth sat down and took my hand in his. "I hate to alarm you any more than you already are, but I can't locate Maggie."

I started toward my phone. "There's a message on my answering machine, maybe she called."

He latched onto my hand. "The call was from LeeAnne. It

229

seems someone has stolen the lockbox she had in her closet."

I slumped back down. "Oh, no. All those lovely things her husband gave her were in that box. She must be devastated."

I pulled myself up again, held my aching head and paced back and forth in front of Lumley. I stomped my foot and screamed, "I have a man in my apartment with an extra hole in his head, LeeAnne's been robbed, and Maggie is missing. we've got to do *something*!"

He stood in front of me to block my exit and placed his hands on my shoulders. The man was getting awfully grabby with my body. "Frankie is with LeeAnne and Jamie is looking for Maggie. There's nothing more we can do until the police arrive. Why don't you sit down, you might have a concussion. An ambulance is on the way."

I pushed him away and my head screamed its dissent of the action. I grabbed my pounding skull again. "Who are you people? And what have you done with my friend?" I collapsed back into my chair, a blubbering bulk of tears and confusion.

Chapter 34

The Man Without a Hat

Elsworth answered the knock at my door; suddenly emergency medical people filled the room and buzzed around me like mosquitoes to blood. They took my vitals, checked my eyes and the knot on my head, and suggested a trip to the ER as a precaution. I turned them down and had to sign a form stating that I refused treatment.

As they exited, my daughter, Emily, showed up, and began carrying on as if the Loblolly strangler had assaulted me. She was dressed in a bright red running suit, her hair was pulled into a ponytail and a sweatband cinched her forehead. She had obviously been in her workout room when Elsworth called. At 5' 8" she wasn't as tall as I, and she worked hard to keep her weight down. To call it an obsession would be an understatement; she attacked exercise with the same single-mindedness as she did everything else in her life. I sighed. It was no wonder her husband had left her. There was no way he could measure up to her rigid standards. Her father had that same 'barge into everything head first' attitude.

"Mother," she said in that high-pitched, accusing voice of hers, "are you alright? Who attacked you? You should really go to the hospital to be properly checked out." She faltered before asking her next question. "Were you physically assaulted?"

I raised my aching head and looked into her concerned eyes. The poor, misguided child did not deserve one of my snide remarks. I reached out and took her hand. "No, darling, Elsworth thinks I might have just bumped my head when I fainted." I glared at Lumley and shook my head so he wouldn't mention the golf club.

"What would cause you to faint? Are you ill?"

Obviously whoever called her had not given Emily the full story. "Sit down, dear." She sat beside me without releasing my hand. When I was sure she was comfortable, I took a deep breath and said, "I found a body behind my couch."

"What?" She jumped up and screamed, "Mother, I'm taking you out of this place. NOW!"She pulled on my arm, but she was no match for my two hundred and forty-five pounds. "Get your things; we're leaving!"

Elsworth took her arm and guided Emily back into the chair. She glared at him. "Are you the person who called me?"

He nodded.

I made the introduction. "Emily, this is Elsworth Lumley. He's one of the good guys, even though he doesn't wear a white hat."

She looked at me as if I'd just gone 'round the bend. I continued, unflustered by "the look". This was Emily's normal way of asserting herself as the dominant female—the only sane, logical member of the family. One of her shrinks probably gave her the idea. She had them all convinced I was some doddering old fool in the last stages of senility. "Elsworth, this is my overprotective daughter, Emily."

They exchanged how-do-you-do's, and she pushed on. "You haven't answered my questions."

Elsworth gave her a rather tired smile. "We don't know at this time exactly who the deceased is, but I don't think he died here."

"You mean someone placed a dead body in my mother's apartment? That's sick. Why would anyone do that?"

Elsworth looked from her to me. "Yes, it is a little sick." He cocked his head in my direction. "I believe your mother may have upset someone who was on the brink of collapse; she became the catalyst that drove the perpetrator over the edge."

I could see he was winning her over. She passed him a sympathetic smile. "That's not difficult to believe," she sighed. "Mother has kept me on the edge for years. Thank God for good therapists!"

"Emily, Mr. Lumley does not want to hear about our family problems, or your mind-altering shrinks."

She spoke to me in the accusing fashion of a mother who wants to know why her child came home with a black eye and torn overalls. "Well, Mother, what did you do to make someone angry enough to deposit a body behind your couch?"

"I'm sure I don't know, dear. And could you keep your voice down? My head hurts, and the folks around here retire early."

The door opened again and in swarmed the police, Frankie and Jamie Cunningham, and two imposing figures in dark suits. Bernie stepped out from behind the guys in suits. He sauntered over and took my free hand; at that point my daughter's mouth dropped open and her chin sagged nearly to her chest. I smiled up at him and thanked him for coming.

Jamie used my phone, and in a few minutes Lennie was at my

door. As he stepped in I could see about fifteen old people in the hall gawking to get a glimpse of the action in my room. I couldn't make them all out, but recognized Marvin Oglevie, Ora Price and Kate and Stanley McGinnis. I glanced around the room; with the exceptions of Annie and Rick, all my suspects seemed to be present and accounted for.

I introduced Emily to Bernie and suggested she go call her brothers. She needed something to do, and I was tired of her reproving stares.

The Cunninghams, Elsworth and the suits had their heads together on the other side of the room. I excused myself to Bernie, asked him to sit down and wait for me, and approached them. Whatever was going on, I intended to be a part of it. With more bravado than actual courage, I said, "I assume, since Maggie is not present, she has not been found."

Frankie took my arm. Everyone around here was sure getting touchy-feely tonight. "No, Helen. I'm afraid not."

I pulled away from her, pointed at the suits and demanded, "Then, I suggest you get these guys here, whoever they are, and go find her before she ends up dead behind somebody's couch!"

The taller of the suits stepped up to me. "We are in charge here. Please step back and let us…"

Elsworth jumped in front of me, grabbed the guy and pulled him to one side. "Graham, you have overstepped your bounds. Let me remind you, Jamie is in charge here. I advise you to not speak to Mrs. Patterson, or anyone else here, for that matter, in that tone of voice again. If you do, I guarantee you will be back at the office filing paperwork until hell freezes over!"

Nice touch. I was impressed. And now I was sure Elsworth

Lumley was a suit, too—or at least had been at one time, if what he said about being retired was true.

While Elsworth was beating Graham down, Jamie signaled to Lennie. "Lennie, take your master key and check all the empty apartments, supply closets, anywhere they might have hidden Mrs. Taylor. Be sure to check the Harris' and Wolf's apartments; they are on vacation."

"Yes, Sir!" Lennie saluted and was out the door.

I asked again, "Who *are* you people?"

Frankie smiled. "We are federal agents. Elsworth will fill you in later. Right now, why don't you go check on your friend, LeeAnne? She was very distraught, and I told her I would send you to sit with her."

I looked at Lumley. He said, "That's a good idea, Helen. We have to finish up the investigation. You won't be able to stay in your apartment for a few days. Perhaps you should go stay with your daughter. The authorities will have some questions, but they can wait."

I shivered at the thought of having to spend the night being psychoanalyzed by Emily, but couldn't think of an alternative since my apartment was off-limits. "You promise you will explain this mess soon?"

He gave me that same tired smile he'd shown Emily earlier. His voice tightened. "I promise as soon as we find Maggie, I'll give the Tricycle Girls the whole story."

I believed him. He really did care about Maggie; I heard it in his voice.

"I'm taking this computer," the obnoxious Graham stated as he began to unplug components from the wall sockets.

I turned to protest, but Elsworth beat me to the punch. His voice had turned to ice. "Graham! What did you say?"

"I'm sorry," he stammered. "Mrs. Patterson, there may be some information on your computer relevant to our case. Would you allow us to take it back to our office and check through your files?"

"That's better," growled Elsworth. He turned to me. "It's merely a precaution. The agency tends to be a bit paranoid of any secret information that may slip into the hands of the unsuspecting public." He smiled. "Once they are assured you have no hidden files or covert information, your computer will be returned."

I shrugged. "I have nothing to hide. The most damning information I have in there is the juicy tidbit about Gladys Butler's dentures in Charlie Arbuckle's medicine cabinet." Everyone except the suits chuckled.

"Excuse me a minute." I walked, a bit unsteadily to my bedroom, pulled the manila folder from its hiding place under my mattress and returned to the circle of suits. "Here is a copy of all my notes on the case." Frankie accepted it with a nod.

Just then the coroner entered our circle. "It appears the deceased is dead from a single bullet to the brain."

Now there was a news flash. I wondered how much a coroner got paid to deliver those lines?

My bravado continued. "Let me guess. You will know more after the autopsy."

He glared at me and ordered the body be hauled away. Tagged and bagged, were his exact words. Officers draped the room with bright yellow ribbon. It might have been festive but for the bold, black lettering labeling my apartment as, **CRIME SCENE. DO NOT CROSS**.

I walked back to where Bernie still sat waiting patiently for my return. "Would you like to walk with me to LeeAnne's? I need to check on her, and I'm trying to avoid my daughter." As he stood up and moved with me toward the door I said, "This will be one more story for Emily to tell her shrink about her 'impossible mother'. I'm not in the mood to listen to her right now."

Bernie patted my hand, but kept his silence.

As we walked hand-in-hand down the hall, I continued. "Emily's not a bad person; she just takes life too seriously. She means well, as all the psychologists would say. But I don't conform to her idea of a 'typical mother'. Never have, and probably never will. And I'm too old to change now."

He smiled up at me and shook his head.

"What?" I asked him.

"I was merely noting the change in you. Your conversational skills are becoming more well-rounded. I remember a time, not too long ago, when a long conversation for you consisted of two words—less, if "Humph" would suffice. At least that was how you dealt with anyone other than Maggie or LeeAnne."

"I guess I am talking too much." I sighed. "It must be the stress of the night. It's not every day one finds a body behind the couch."

"And thank goodness for that. If my opinion counts, I think you're holding up marvelously under the circumstances. And as I told you before, I like the sound of your voice."

I patted his arm. "Thank you, Bernie. You've been a good friend. Ahh, here we are."

I knocked on LeeAnne's door. "LeeAnne, it's me, Helen. Bernie and I came to check on you."

She opened the door a crack and I could tell she had been crying. She let us in and wrapped me in a hug so tight it nearly took my breath away. Bernie followed, and while LeeAnne filled me in on her loss, he made tea and brought us each a cup.

LeeAnne smiled. "Why, Bernie, how sweet. Now sit down, you two, and tell me what's going on around here."

I told her about the body in my room, my fall, the feds and the confiscation of my computer. She gasped in all the right places. It wouldn't make up for the loss of her jewelry, but I at least managed to distract her from that loss for a while.

When I had finished the story, complete with embellishments, including the fact my place was now a crime scene and temporarily off limits, she said, "I have a wonderful idea. You can stay here in my apartment." She patted the couch. "This loveseat pulls out into a single bed. You need a place to stay, and I would feel so much better having someone here with me."

Bernie spoke up. "Sounds like the perfect solution." He sipped the last of his tea. "And you won't have to deal with answering your daughter's questions—at least for tonight. Now, if you lovely ladies will excuse me, I will take my leave so you can settle down for the evening. Unless," he looked wistfully at me, "there's anything else I can do for you."

I smiled at him. "Well, since LeeAnne invited me to stay here, I do need to go back to my place and get a few things. I would prefer to not go alone. Could you walk me back to my place?"

"Certainly. I would be honored to see you get safely there and back."

We returned to my place for the necessities and informed

Elsworth and crew where I could be reached. Emily was adamant that I not spend one more night in this place, but my stubbornness trumped hers and I won out. I guess she didn't get all her temperament from her father. Bernie, good as his word, saw me safely back to LeeAnne's. There was one awkward moment as we stood outside her door. He reached up, took my face in his hands and, I think, was about to kiss me, when LeeAnne opened the door. He immediately dropped his hands to his sides.

Oblivious to the interruption, she said, "I thought I heard you out here. Noises all seem magnified after a scare like this. Come on in. I want to get this place locked up." Suddenly it dawned on her that she may have broken in on an intimate moment, and she stammered, "Oh, I'm sorry, you two. Let me close the door so you can say your goodnights."

I put my hand on the door. "It's alright, LeeAnne. We've said our goodnights. See you tomorrow, Bernie, and thanks again." I wasn't ready for full-on mouth kissing, anyway.

Chapter 35

The Party's Over

The incessant ringing of a phone woke me; I rolled over to grab it and nearly fell off the bed. I reached for my bedside lamp and realized I was not in my own room. Where was I? It was pitch black, and I still wasn't able to find a confounded lamp.

Suddenly light flooded the room from an overhead fixture, and LeeAnne stood in front of me, untamed red hair flying around her drawn features. "That was Elsworth. Lennie found Maggie in the maintenance shed."

I grabbed my chest and gasped, "Is she…" I couldn't bring myself to say the word 'dead'.

She sat down beside me and shook her head. "She's alive, but she was bound and gagged. Elsworth says she's fine. He's taking her to the hospital to be checked for exposure and dehydration. He said he'd come see us as soon as they get back."

I ran my fingers through my hair, felt the sore knot on my skull, and tried, unsuccessfully, to wipe the grogginess out of my brain. "Thank God. What time is it?"

"Four-forty-five. Poor Maggie must have been tied up out

there for hours. I'll bet she was terrified."

I nodded, still in shock, but glad Maggie had been found. "I'm glad Lumley took her to the hospital. Maggie has a touch of high blood pressure. The stress could have caused a stroke or a heart attack." I buried my face in my hands. "What was I thinking when I exposed my friends to such danger? It was just a crazy game; I never thought anyone would get hurt."

LeeAnne put her arm over my shoulder. "You can't blame yourself, Helen. It's not your fault. We're all grown-ups, and we were all playing a game. Unfortunately, we didn't realize the other parties were playing for real."

I stood up and started to pace. "Lumley tried to warn me, but I didn't believe him. Solving crimes is always so easy in mystery novels. Those things should come with a warning: "Do not try this at home!""

"For Maggie's sake, don't you think it's time you started calling him Elsworth, instead of Lumley? Do you really think he's a fed?"

I stopped pacing and nodded. "The way he was barking orders, I'm sure of it. He sure put that Graham fellow in his place. That's one thing I was right about, anyway."

I went to her kitchen and began opening cabinet doors. "Do you have any coffee? There's no way we're going to get back to sleep; we might as well be full of caffeine when Maggie and Elsworth get here."

LeeAnne made a pot of coffee and we discussed possible scenarios for the solution of our crime.

We decided that Annie and Rick must be involved, but couldn't figure out what the feds had to do with them. Dumpy

Annie didn't look like a crook or a killer. And Rick could really cook! I'd hate to lose him as the chef of this place. What would I have to look forward to without his scrumptious desserts? Annie, on the other hand, would be no great loss; I didn't join in her little programs anyway. Still, neither LeeAnne nor I could picture either of them as international threats.

"I was so sure the Cunninghams were behind everything, I really didn't take the rest of our suspects seriously," I moaned.

We talked our way through the pot of coffee and still had loads of unanswered questions. LeeAnne cleared the cups from the table. "Guess we'll just have to wait and see what Elsworth says. But if Annie and Rick are behind this, they are a dangerous pair, whether they look the part or not. After all, they murdered some poor guy and locked Maggie up in the shed."

I checked the clock. Six a.m. It was still too early to go to the dining room; besides, with Rick on the run, who was going to cook? Murder and mayhem notwithstanding, my stomach said someone needed to prepare breakfast!

We decided to get dressed; Maggie and Lumley— Elsworth—should be along soon. I paced the floor again until LeeAnne joked that I was wearing ruts in her carpeting. They finally showed up and the three of us hugged and cried and hugged some more. I apologized for getting Maggie in the middle of my craziness. She repeated what LeeAnne had said about us all being adults and just not realizing we were getting in over our heads.

I held her at arm's length and asked, "So, how are you really doing?"

Elsworth draped his arm protectively over her shoulder.

"The doctor said except for a bit of elevated blood pressure and slight dehydration, I'm fine." She hugged me again and smiled. "He said to drink lots of liquids to replace my electrolytes, but I'm none the worse for wear. It was, however, very frightening in that shed. I had to keep reminding myself that the worst that could happen is that Lennie wouldn't find me until tomorrow when he had to get the mower out to do the lawn. He does it every Saturday."

"Annie knew that too. Even though she was trying to frighten us, she must have known Maggie would be found soon," said LeeAnne.

"You can give her the benefit of a doubt if you want," huffed Elsworth. "As far as I'm concerned, they don't deserve any consideration." Anger and frustration showed in his face and his voice. "I must admit, though, it could have turned out a lot worse." He pulled Maggie close again, as if he was afraid she might disappear if he let go.

He continued, "We knew Annie and Rick were behind the whole scheme, but Annie really flipped out at the last."

He pointed to me. "There were some strands of hair on that golf club. It looks as though you were struck with it Helen, probably just as you passed out. Fortunately for you, she didn't get a good swing at your head as you fell, and had to make a quick get-away before I showed up."

I shivered. "Was she there to kill me?"

"I think," said Elsworth, "she and Rick came to deposit the body as a warning, and you showed up before she had a chance to get out of your apartment. You happened to be, as they say, in the wrong place at the wrong time."

"But," said LeeAnne, "they had already kidnapped Maggie by then. Why did they do that?"

"I suspect it was another warning."

"So," I said, "you promised a full explanation as soon as Maggie was found. Tell us the whole story."

Maggie grinned. Obviously Lumley—Elsworth—had filled her in already. "Come on down to the dining room. El and the others are going to make a statement to everyone at the same time."

LeeAnne and I followed 'El' and Maggie out the door and down the hall. Bernie was waiting at the entrance to the dining room.

"Nearly everyone has arrived," he said to Elsworth.

I stared at him. "Were you in on this, too?"

He dropped into step with me. "Elsworth asked me to go round up everyone for an emergency meeting before breakfast. I don't have a clue as to what's going on, I just do as I'm told."

"Good man," I smiled at him.

He winked, pulled out chairs for LeeAnne and me and sat down between us. Elsworth helped Maggie into her chair and stood behind her, his hands on her shoulders, gently massaging her neck.

The Cunninghams strode to the front of the group; Jamie raised his hands to quiet the murmurings of the crowd. "Good morning. Thank you all for coming out so early. We decided an explanation was in order to all of you about the strange things that have been going on around here. First, I would like to introduce myself. You all know me as Jamie Cunningham, accountant. I am, in fact, FBI agent James Carmichael, and Miss Cunningham," he gestured to Frankie, "is my partner, not my wife—as wonderful as that association might be." A smile and nod from Frankie and chuckles from the crowd.

Jamie pointed in our direction. "Elsworth Lumley is one of our distinguished retired agents. We asked for his help on this case since he was already in place here and his presence wouldn't cause suspicion.

"As you know," he continued, "some strange things have been happening around here for the last few months, not the least of which was the replacement of your administrator, George Hardestee. The first order of business today is to tell you George will be back as your administrator starting immediately."

There was thunderous applause from the crowd. George materialized from somewhere and smiled and waved.

Jamie went on, "His job was never in jeopardy; he was, in fact, working with the Federal Government in an operation to catch some international jewel thieves. The woman you all know as Annie James and her accomplice, whom you know as Rick Garrison, were wanted for several jewel thefts. They had fallen off the radar, and we had no idea where they were. A tip came in to our office that they were living here in Loblolly, and we tracked them down to Golden Harvest. Mr. Hardestee very graciously agreed to let us come in to try to apprehend the pair. Had we known the two were so desperate that they would turn to violence, we would have taken steps to apprehend them sooner.

"It's fortunate that no one here was seriously hurt, although Maggie Taylor spent a very uncomfortable and frightening night in the maintenance shed, and Helen Patterson was evidently assaulted with a golf club. Mr. Lumley tells me Maggie is recovering nicely." He waved to Elsworth. "I leave her in your capable hands."

Elsworth returned the wave and hugged Maggie tighter.

Jamie addressed me. "How are you feeling today, Mrs. Patterson?"

I stood and rubbed my head. "Fortunately for me, I was hit on my hard head, so there's no damage done."

Everyone chuckled as I intended. Always go for the laugh, is my motto.

"That's good," said Jamie. "Frankie and I will be leaving later today. We want to thank you all for your help and for accepting us here." He addressed me again. "Mrs. Patterson, your notes on the case were very comprehensive, but next time you decide to solve a crime, be a bit more cautious, okay?"

I nodded and sat down.

He continued, "Are there any questions from the audience before I turn the podium over to George?"

"Have you found our things?" someone asked.

"We have recovered the items," Jamie said. "Some were still here locked in Annie's file cabinet, along with the thousand dollars from the talent show. The rest of the items were in the apartment they shared in town. They hadn't had a chance to find a fence to dispose of anything."

Sandy Germain raised her hand. "When will we get our things back? Or will we?"

"The items that were stolen from the residents will have to remain in evidence temporarily. Everything will be returned as soon as the case is made against the pair. If you had something taken, please come see Frankie or myself so we can get an inventory of your missing items. Anyone who would like a receipt can get one at that time.

"Any other questions?"

I raised my hand. "When is breakfast, and who is going to cook?"

Jamie smiled. "Leave it to you, Helen, to get down to the basics. As a matter of fact, breakfast is being catered today by the Wheel House, and comes compliments of the U.S. government. However, don't expect that to continue."

Whistles and applause erupted from the audience again.

George took the stage and thanked us all for our patience, and the FBI for closing the case. He then added, "Frankie, Jamie and Mr. Lumley all told me that some very good sleuthing was done by three of our residents. Will Helen Patterson, Maggie Taylor and LeeAnne Warner please stand?" We all stood up, pleasantly embarrassed by the attention.

Frankie stepped up beside George. "The FBI wants to commend these three ladies for their persistence and accuracy in following the clues in this case. Their diligence matched that of any good agent."

There was hearty applause and someone piped up, "Do they get to call themselves junior G-men, now?" More laughter.

Frankie smiled. "I'm sure they would rather be called the Tricycle Girls. After all, that's what their business cards say. Thanks, ladies."

She left the stage and George exclaimed, "Let's eat!"

Epilogue
All Wrapped Up

Two days later the five of us, the Tricycle Girls plus Bernie and Elsworth, sat in the library discussing the latest articles laid out before us. The case seemed to have hit all the major newspapers. Bernie had one spread out on the table in front of him. "It seems, Helen, your body…"

I shuddered, "Please don't call it my body; that implies that I am somehow responsible for it."

"OK," he said. "The body which was discovered behind your couch—is that better?"

I nodded.

"His name was Eddie Small—Little Eddie on the street. He was a small-time, pardon the pun, crook and safecracker. According to this article, Annie and Rick *allegedly* hired him to crack a safe—LeeAnne's, and probably any others they happened to find in the apartments. When they discovered LeeAnne had only a lockbox they could carry away, they told him they didn't need his services. He demanded payment for his time, showed up here and threatened to rat them out if he wasn't paid. Annie went ballistic—literally—and shot him."

248

"Poor man," I said.

LeeAnne spoke up. "He was not a 'poor man', Helen. He was a crook. Although that doesn't mean he deserved to be shot." She looked at Elsworth. "But why put the body in Helen's apartment?"

He shrugged. "It's hard to say. Annie had pretty much lost all reason by then. I'm only speculating, but she possibly wanted to leave Helen another message like the two threatening letters."

LeeAnne and Maggie looked from Lumley to me. "What threatening letters?" Maggie asked. "I never heard about any threatening letters!"

I waved my hand in the air. "It was nothing. I'll tell you about it later."

"Not later. Now!" demanded my best friend. If I withheld any more evidence I might jeopardize our lifelong friendship. I explained about the letters cut out of magazines, then hurriedly changed the subject. "What did you find in that paper, Maggie? Anything good?"

She frowned at me, and I knew I hadn't heard the end of this evidence-withholding business. She shook open the paper in her hands. "Here's a picture of them after the arrest at the apartment they shared. Wow, Annie doesn't look too happy."

We all gathered around her. The grainy photo was of a sulking Rick Garrison and a wild-eyed, wild-haired woman. Maggie read the caption:

"International jewel thieves, Annie James, AKA Diamond Girl Jamison, and long-time accomplice, Ricardo Garrisoni, being led away by federal agents." She squinted at the photo. "I don't see Jamie or Frankie in the picture."

Using my newfound introductory FBI skills, I said, "They

probably didn't want to be photographed. It would compromise their ability to work undercover."

Everyone except Elsworth agreed that was a plausible answer. He kept his silence and smiled.

"What else does the article say," asked LeeAnne.

Maggie continued to read:

'When questioned by this reporter, Ms. Jamison burst into some song to the tune of Daisy, Daisy. The exact words were garbled, but she screamed to print them exactly as she sang them:

"Hell-on, Maggot, Le-on and dum-de-de.

I've gone crazy trying to get rid of thee."

I shook my head. "Poor, crazed woman."

"Don't feel sorry for her, Helen," said LeeAnne. "Remember, she tried to smash your head in with that golf club."

I nodded. "Yeah, it's a good thing she's a lousy golfer."

"Leave it to you to make a joke out of nearly being killed," said Maggie. She continued reading:

"The next words the suspect spoke or, more literally, sang, were indecipherable, but the last bizarre line before Ms. Jamison burst into hysterical laughter, was something about a bicycle built for three. Ms. Jamison's attorney will no doubt plead insanity and hope for a sympathetic jury."

Maggie put the paper down and looked at me. "Helen, I think you drove the woman over the edge with your investigation."

I groaned. Emily would no doubt have a heyday with this information. Perhaps she would even go see Annie and give her the name of a good shrink.

Bernie took my hand. "So, Helen, are the Tricycle Girls still in business?"

"No!" shouted Maggie.

"Never again," concurred LeeAnne.

"That's too bad," he said, "because Elsworth and I took the liberty of having some tokens made up for you three sleuths." He reached into his pocket and pulled out two small boxes, handed one to me and one to LeeAnne. Lumley held out a box to Maggie.

I opened mine and held up a bracelet with two small charms—a golf club and a tricycle. I patted Bernie's arm. "How thoughtful, Bernie."

He blushed. "Just a reminder of your help in catching the jewel thieves."

I elbowed him in the ribs. "Yeah. We old jewels solved the case of missing old jewels."

"We're not that old!" LeeAnne said. She opened her box and squealed, "Look, everyone! Mine has a little microphone and a tricycle. Isn't that sweet?" She gave Bernie a hug. "What does yours have, Maggie?"

Maggie laughed as she held up her bracelet. Along with the tricycle was a small figure. "Where in the world did you find a Wonder Woman charm, El?"

"It wasn't easy; but you can find pretty much anything on the internet."

"Now that we've got these beautiful bracelets to fill up, the Tricycle Girls may have to ride again," I said.

Maggie and LeeAnne both rolled their eyes.

I jumped up. "Anyone for ice cream to celebrate?"

"Yes," they all chimed in.

"Let's go, then."

I linked my right hand through Bernie's extended arm and

hooked my left into LeeAnne's. El and Maggie followed close behind, hand-in-hand. I began a loud, off-key rendition of *Daisy*, and my four friends joined in as we headed out the door. I smiled down at Bernie as we sang, *"I'm half crazy, all for the love of you."*

Never say never.

The End

If you enjoyed

OLD JEWELS,

please take a moment to leave
a review at your favorite retailer.

Thank You

Pat Pratt

Coming Soon

Another adventure of the Tricycle Girls

NO STONE UNTURNED

Helen Patterson and her fellow Tricycle Girls, Maggie Taylor and LeeAnne Warner, embark on a week-long excursion to Stone Mountain, Georgia with other members of Golden Harvest, where they all reside. Along the way they encounter unwanted guests, unsavory characters, murder, and mayhem.

Helen and the girls have one week to catch the killer. The list of suspects is long, and Helen is right at the top because of her 60-year-old history with the deceased. They must solve the crime because all agree Helen would not look good in horizontal stripes.